Sherry - Aug '05

DAKOTA REBEL

Dakota Rebel

Lynn Dell

Crystal Prism: Reflections of Love
An Enrapture Book

Published by New Age Dimensions, Inc.
Publishing For The World's New Age

CRYSTAL PRISM REFLECTIONS OF LOVE An Enrapture Book
An Imprint and line of NEW AGE DIMENSIONS, INC.
P.O. Box 772097
Coral Springs, FL 33077

Cover Design by Melissa Alvarez
Published by arrangement with the author.
ISBN 1-59611-012-0
www.NewAgeDimensionsPublishing.com

First New Age Dimensions Trade Paperback Printing: July 2004
10 9 8 7 6 5 4 3 2 1

To all the Dakotaland farmers and ranchers, past, present and future.

The best to you,
Lynn Allene

Chapter One

Dakota Territory, 1874

Rebecca unfastened two more buttons on the shirt that clung to her moist skin. She was exposing more of her small breasts than was proper, but modesty had no place here. She and Madam were the only ones around for miles. Besides, the air on her bare flesh felt wonderful.

"My, Madam, it sure is sultry. It's got to be the most hot and humid day in all my twenty-two years!" Rebecca said.

Madam silently regarded her with large, soulful eyes. Her lumbering body strained to pull the wagon onward.

The relentless Dakota sun blistered down on them without mercy. Perspiration stung Rebecca's eyes; beads of it rolled into the small of her back. A few strands of copper-streaked brown hair stuck wetly to her neck.

The girl stooped, hefted the nearest bundle of oats, and tossed it onto the growing pile in the cart. The golden heap swayed with every movement of the creaking wagon. Rebecca held a pair of reins loosely in the lean, tanned fingers of one hand.

"Whoa, girl!" she said to her companion. Madam's fawn-colored flanks were dark with sweat; cow-smell mixed with the scent of wet leather in Rebecca's nostrils.

Rebecca dropped the sticky reins and pressed her hands into the small of her back. She arched her body, trying to stretch out the kinks that came from frequent bending. She felt giddy looking at the pure, clean ocean of sky. At the horizon, the perfect blue paled to a crystalline color. No rain clouds in sight.

In the last two weeks alone she had cut the oat crop with a sickle, gathered it carefully, and tied it into bundles. She'd propped the yellow sheaves upright in the field. Now she was ready to store them in the granary. Her accomplishments over the past season were many, and each one had been essential.

Madam stretched, then stomped a foot at the biting flies crawling on her legs. Rebecca's gaze roamed over her land appreciatively. Father had done well in finding and procuring this acreage near the James River. Surrounded by smooth hills—the petite, rolling kind that follows a river—the homestead was a serene, private spot. The earthen soddy, barn and sheds nestled, secluded, between slopes to the west and north and the sinuous river at the south and east.

Birds called keenly from the water's edge. *This place is precious,* Rebecca thought fiercely, *and it's all up to me to keep it.*

It greatly riled her how several greedy codgers—Starns, for one, and old Mr. Aarsen, too—had tried to seize her spread when she inherited it four years ago. Rebecca wrinkled her nose in disgust at the though of them. She was young and female, and they'd believed she was vulnerable.

Rebecca swept off her wide-brimmed straw hat and felt a breeze evaporate the sweat from her forehead. She gazed at her work partner and her heart went out to the animal.

"When we finish, I'm going to tie you to the shady side of the barn and give you a good rubdown, Madam. You deserve it!" The cow merely flicked her ears.

Rebecca smashed the hat on again and grimaced at the touch of the damp, clammy band on her brow. How she wished for one of her old thin cotton skirts—how splendidly cool it would feel! The heavy trousers she wore now were—*Oh, stop that sorry thinking.*

Looking ahead, Rebecca counted the bundles still standing. Only ten more, thank goodness. She clucked to Madam to move to the next sheaf of oats.

Her mind wandered again as she worked . . . and a familiar loneliness crept in. "I, Rebecca Marie LaRoche, am in dire need of a man!"

She let her eyes range around the property again and quietly added, as if to excuse her rash words of a moment before, "There's a lot of work a man could do around here."

And she knew just the right man. Cooper, they called him at the mill. When Rebecca first saw him there, for a heartbeat their eyes had met and held—one second, two. His thick, black, wavy hair framed an angular face. His dark, deep-set eyes looked intelligent, curious. She knew now that he probably gave every woman he met that probing look. His potent brown eyes appeared to see deep inside a woman's soul, and his smile was most provocative.

The memory of him made her ache with longing. With a sigh she turned to the last bundle. In one motion she picked it up and threw it atop the teetering pile on the cart. Then she turned Madam toward home; slowly the two of them made their way.

Rebecca recalled again that intense, eye-locking first sight of Cooper when she was eighteen. He'd just arrived in the Yankton area when he began working at the gristmill. She never did hear his last name, and she knew nothing more about him. Oh, but the feelings he stirred up inside her just by the sight of him!

She spoke aloud to the ungainly cow, to the empty sky, "I'm afraid Cooper isn't even aware of me. Anyway, I'd be the *last* girl in his dreams. I'm not all soft and tempting—there's nothing womanly about me. I would have made a better boy!"

Rebecca wondered whether she'd be alone on this homestead forever. The home place she was trying so hard to keep, for herself and for the sake of her parents.

Near the granary she unhitched Madam, who mooed plaintively. She tethered the cow in the shade, watered her, and began to rub her down with a rag. Rebecca's mind strayed back to the Sunday she'd last gone to church.

"Madam, I remember how the lovely Liza Wright draped herself all over Cooper, right there in front of everyone! No shame."

The cow's tail flicked back and forth, swatting at the flies on her loins.

"And, dear girl, that same day in church, she and that snooty Angela were whispering right in front of me, knowing full well I could hear them." Rebecca pitched her voice high and sneered, mimicking Angela. "Rebecca LaRoche is so mannish. She'll stay an old maid always. No man would ever wish to plant himself in her bed."

Madam threw her head back and touched her moist nose to her shoulder.

Rebecca's mind drifted amongst her gloomy thoughts as she stroked Madam's soft coat. Her notions clung to her like the bits of straw that stuck to her damp arms and made them itch horribly. She brushed them off, thoughts and straw alike, and turned back to the cart to unload the oat bundles into the granary. The sun slipped under a cloud just as she finished. More clouds scudded along the west ridge—

murky ones, moving fast.

She knew very well how quickly things could change on the prairie. One moment one's life course seemed set, and the next everything was different.

Now an angry storm approached like rumbling runaway horses.

Rebecca hated storms. They frightened her, especially the battering winds. Now she heard resounding thunderclaps in the distance.

She hurried to Madam, untied her lead, and clucked at her to move. But the slumberous creature had put in a long day's work. She stretched and then stubbornly planted her feet. Finally Rebecca coaxed and tugged her to the sharp-edged ravine several hundred feet beyond the barn. Years ago her father had made a dugout into the steep bank there. He'd built a lean-to over it for added protection. Now Rebecca harbored her cow there.

She ran back to the barn for the hogs. Though she lured them with a bucket of feed, the agitated animals squealed and scattered. Rebecca shouted and stomped her feet desperately to chase them into the enclosure. A burst of wind sent her hat sailing away, and more snappy gusts whipped at her hair and clothing. The blazing day had turned dark and cold. The poultry would have to make do in their chicken house, she thought grimly.

When she'd secured the animals, Rebecca hastily made her way to the cabin. Inside, she gathered together several quilts, the lantern, a canteen of water, and lucifers. All these she left in the middle of the floor near the trap door to the root cellar.

Then she heard it. A rumble louder than mere thunder. The tempest buffeted the soddy tumultuously and caused dirt to sift down onto her shoulders and into her hair. Rebecca flung open the trap door, her heart thumping frantically. She struck a match and held it to the lantern wick. She scooped the quilts and canteen into the black hole, held the lantern in her left hand and used her right to descend the ladder. Ordinarily, she didn't like going into the loam-scented cellar, but now she scurried.

Once down, Rebecca made a place for herself between a crock of lard and a wooden box of carrots packed in sand. The earthy scent of potatoes and turnips was pleasant enough, but the dirt walls and floor smelled musty and the air felt damp. Overhead, cobwebs occupied the corners. Her skin crawled as she imagined salamanders slithering, snakes wiggling, lizards creeping, and spiders crawling all over her bare skin.

* * *

The two cowboys rode on in silence, nervously eyeing the ominous black sky. The older of the two, Yago, wore his hat low; he'd tied it down to keep the punishing wind from stealing it. His fairer brother was hatless, long blond hair lashing about his freckled face.

Yago's greatest fear, more than foul weather, was to come upon a party of warring Indians. So far their luck held. They'd rarely made a fire except to cook some beans and coffee. Sometimes, the two of them just chewed on dried jerky. They were into the fourteenth day of their journey and close to their destination.

They'd spied several bears from afar, high up in the Black Hills. The beasts lumbered among the evergreens, their reddish coats flashing briefly in the sun. Another danger, rattlers, had been an everyday affair for the travelers earlier. But they'd encountered none of the deadly snakes for days now, since they'd crossed the Missouri.

The treeless plains had broiled and shimmered in oppressive heat all day long; now this fearsome evening was setting in. Yago glanced at the slight figure of his little brother hunched over in his saddle. He hoped they would spot a homestead, and soon.

A dreadful crack of lightning punctuated his thoughts. Hell, he'd settle for any shelter for the night. The lowering sky, with its crashing noise and blinding flashes of lightning, seemed like one big package of Chinese firecrackers!

Malachi was so green, untried. Yago never should have allowed him to come. *"I will not rest until you are safely home,"* their mother had said. *How did I get roped into bringing the kid.*

He knew exactly how it had happened. . . .

* * *

Martina Conrad had directed her daughter and two youngest sons to meet her in the study of their expansive ranch home. She sat rigidly at her late husband's wide, heavy desk. Her eyes were such a deep brown that they were nearly black, and they expressed her every emotion eloquently. Her carefully-chosen words were spoken gently in the Hispanic accent of her heritage. "It has been three weeks since your father's death."

She stopped, swallowed. "When your father passed away so unexpectedly, it was a shock for all of us. David Dunn, his lawyer, approached me in town today. He asked me whether enough time has passed since the burial that he might read me the will left for us by your father. Most of it was as I expected, but a small part of it was a *sorpresa*—it surprised me!"

She turned her dark head to her daughter. "Chalina, my rose, I will start with you. You are very well provided for. Father left you a dowry of fifty thousand dollars."

A whistle escaped from Malachi's lips.

"For you boys," Martina continued, "the ranch will be divided equally between the three of you. How it will be divided is outlined in the will. A stipulation reads that Cooper must be living here on the ranch and be married within two years of your father's death. I believe it is only fair for him to have that chance.

"But it depends on whether you are able to find Cooper. If you do, there is no reason he cannot return and claim what belongs to him by birthright."

Yago spoke up. "I'm surprised Papa included him at all, the way they constantly tore at each other's throats."

Martina shook her head, swaying the glossy dark brown hair that cascaded down her back like the waves of a gently rolling sea.

"Luke understood his eldest son very well," she said. "He knew Cooper liked being in the company of pretty young ladies, but he knew also of his resolution to stay a bachelor. Your father realized how stubborn and strong-willed Cooper could be, and yet he was aware of how much his eldest loves this ranch and his family."

Chalina questioned her mother, "How can he love this ranch and our family when he willfully stays away for four years?"

"Oh, he does, there is no doubt in my mind about that," Martina said. "Luke and Cooper were too much alike, with the difference of a generation separating their ideas. I was surprised by your father's arrangements at first, but as I have thought about it, I must agree; this is for Cooper's own good. This way there will be true Conrad children to inherit his share of the estate. How else would he breed anything but bastards?"

"For his own good. Poor Coop," sighed Chalina.

"Where will we go, to find him?" asked Malachi.

"Oh, Micah!" Chalina cried, using her brother's nickname. "It could take years to locate him. We haven't a clue where to look. He could be anywhere in the world!"

Micah's amber eyes met his sister's dark brown eyes in mutual apprehension. He was sixteen and fair-haired, as his father had been. He had the makings to be a handsome man someday, but for now the boy showed through. The youngest of the children, he possessed a sweet, kind nature.

"I have been receiving letters from Cooper at Christmas-time for four years now," Martina said. "They have all come from the same place, Yankton, in the southeastern part of the Dakota Territory."

"Letters? From Cooper? Why didn't you tell the rest of us about them?" asked Yago. His voice had a cross, indignant edge to it. Born two years after Cooper, he felt very close to him. He too, was tawny-skinned but more husky than his older and younger siblings.

"Now, Yago," Martina said, "I did this so your father would not find out. If he had known, he would have forced Cooper to come back. Their constant quarreling would have been a burden to us all. I thought time and distance would change their attitudes toward each other." Her face crumpled.

"I never dreamed Luke would be taken from us so suddenly. Thrown from his horse. Killed—" Her voice cracked. She broke off, teary-eyed.

Martina collected herself

"Come look, all of you. I have a plan." They gathered around the large desk, and she spread out a map. She pointed with a long delicate finger, first indicating their location in the northeast corner of Wyoming Territory. She swept her hand diagonally, far to the lower right.

"Here is the settlement called Yankton, a river town on the Missouri, the capital of the region. It is a ride of several weeks," Martina said. Concern caused her voice to waver. She stopped, drew from her reserve of self-control, and continued. "Cooper is in this area. He must be found and told. The choice is his if he wishes to come back."

She looked at both her boys in turn.

"When can the two of you be ready?"

"There's some danger involved," Yago said. He looked at Micah. "You think you're old enough?"

"You're not going to deny me this because of my age!" retorted Micah.

"You are a bit young to be going on a journey like this," Martina admitted, as if thinking aloud. "And perhaps I am asking a lot of Yago by sending you along." She turned to her middle son. "But I would worry more, Yago, if you were alone. This is a family matter, to be handled by family. I will worry until all my boys are back again." She asked Yago, "How soon can you go?"

"First light in the morning. Micah, you'd better turn in. I want to study this map and choose the safest route."

"Aw, come on. Quit treating me like a big baby!"

"All right, you can help me plan our course, but you'd better look lively tomorrow morning!" Yago said.

Martina and her daughter left the study with matching worried looks on their faces. The two young men stayed up for some time discussing the trails they would take. Yago knew it would seem an exciting adventure to Micah, but Yago was fraught with tension.

Early the next morning Yago strode into Micah's room to wake him, but the boy was up already. His face glowed with enthusiasm. Before breakfast the two of them readied their provisions, two pack horses and their saddle horses.

Martina stood at the threshold of her home, Chalina

at her side. The two women, one a youthful replica of the other, watched the boys approach the gate.

Martina's hands trembled as she pressed some greenbacks into Yago's palm. "Try to avoid trouble."

"We won't go looking for it, don't worry," Yago said in an effort to reassure his mother.

"You have your guns, do you not?"

"Yes, Ma," Micah answered impatiently.

"I will not rest until you are safely home," she said.

* * *

"I will not rest until you are safely home." His mother and sister had continued to stand there in the doorway, waving, until they had rounded the turn.

Suddenly a shout interrupted Yago's retrospection.

"Here! Look on the other side of the river!" Micah pointed through a break in the trees.

About a half-mile away, a structure nestled into the other side of the valley. It could be their sanctuary for the night! They spurred their horses down the hillside and into knee-high water. From there they struggled into a thick, dense grove of trees, where mosquitoes hummed in their ears and attacked their faces heartlessly.

The horses fought their way through underbrush tangled with wild grapevines, and then through tall native hemp and other grasses. Finally out on a flat of newly-harvested oats they came, racing toward the cabin. Hail pummeled the bent backs of the riders.

"Oh, my God! Micah, look! It's a whirlwind, a . . . a tornado!" Yago had never before seen the strange swirling phenomenon, but he'd heard about it. He and Micah stared with fascination at the rotating cloud beneath a dark mass. A misty, snake-like tail appeared.

"Let's get these horses moving!" Yago cried. They were halfway to their destination when the funnel began to descend.

There could be no pity now for the already-tired animals, but they sensed the danger and needed no prodding. By the time they reached the cabin the tornado column, now a thick, coiling dark mass, had touched down. The boys leaped from their saddles and raced for safety. Free of their riders, the horses galloped off to find their own shelter.

Inside, the open trap door drew Yago's eyes.

"Micah, down here," he ordered. Micah immediately swung himself into the hole and Yago followed, pulling the trap door shut as he descended.

Chapter Two

The cellar spooked Rebecca and the deafening roar outside stirred her nerves to a fever pitch. Then she heard the clomping of boots overhead, and her heart flipped over. Two intruders in her home! They had begun to lower themselves into the cellar when she barked loudly, "Who are you? What do you want?"

The figures on the ladder stiffened.

"Speak up," Rebecca ordered shakily, wishing she sounded more commanding.

"We're just looking for shelter!" The uppermost stranger's voice sounded harsh, sharp.

Rebecca motioned for them to get down and crouch against the wall. She peered at them warily in the flickering lamplight. The smaller, paler one appeared to be an adolescent. Freckles were strewn across his short, wide nose. Thick sandy brows framed fresh, wide-set amber eyes. He looked alert, excited. The other fellow, more mature, was stocky and dark. She guessed him to be about her age. He wore a grave expression on his plain face.

Above, unearthly sounds grew louder. Blaring and shrieking surrounded them. The floorboards vibrated as an unthinkable force ripped at them. Rebecca could hardly breathe. The powerful wind seemed to yank the very air from her lungs. The soddy creaked and groaned under its incredible fury. The driving energy sucked open the trap door and tore at the flooring above their heads.

Then, just as quickly as the barrage had come, it was gone. Cold rain pelted the few remaining floorboards and drizzled onto the three huddled in the dirt. Rebecca threw one of her quilts to the two strangers and they covered themselves as best they could, huddling together.

"We're mighty obliged to you, ma'am. I'm Yago, and this here's my brother, Malachi."

"But you can call me Micah," the boy interjected. "Everybody does."

The two nodded at her and she returned the gesture without speaking.

* * *

Eventually the rain slowed to a light drip, then stopped. Late afternoon sunlight began to filter through the openings left by the devastating storm. It was over.

Yago studied the young woman, trying to interpret her emotional state. He couldn't read her olive green eyes, framed by long dark lashes. Her nose, neither large nor small, was minutely aquiline. Yago liked the way her hair hung past her shoulders sleek and smooth. Glossy brown with a blend of golden and reddish strands, it seemed untouched by the storm. Her full mouth betrayed no reactions to what she'd just experienced.

He thought her small, slim body looked like a boy's in that homespun shirt and corduroy trousers far too large on her. His eyes fell to her dusty ankle-high men's brogans.

She stood haltingly. Looking upward, she dropped the quilt even as she shivered.

Yago understood her hesitation. After all, what remained of this homestead? He realized she wanted to climb the ladder even though she surely dreaded what she would find.

* * *

Rebecca willed herself to scale the steps and peer over the edge. A red sun shone through the broken clouds low in the western sky. When she clambered out, total destruction assaulted her eyes. She saw emptiness where her home had been. The barn, the privy, everything gone, just swept away! Bits of household debris lay scattered about, a tin cup here, a kettle there, half-buried in mud. Ten yards away, a bedraggled hen stood on a fragment of wreckage, her feathers askew. The strong scent of wet earth and crushed vegetation turned Rebecca's stomach.

She felt empty inside as she woodenly made her way through the devastation that had been her domain. The pigs' enclosure had been obliterated. Several chickens lay dead.

Then Rebecca thought of Madam and her stomach jerked violently with sobs that hadn't yet formed tears. She threaded her way around the ruins and toward the ravine. Relief flooded her when she saw the lean-to intact, and big-eyed Madam peering out at her.

Tears came then in a moaning, wracking deluge. She sat on a patch of wet grass with her arms wrapped around her knees, hugging them close to her body as if they, too, would be taken from her. Rocking herself back and forth, she couldn't concentrate on any one thing for long. Her tormented thoughts ran pell-mell through her mind uncontrolled. She had forgotten all about the strangers.

* * *

Yago, a quilt in hand, had followed Rebecca out of the cellar. He'd watched the spiritless girl take in the disaster so stiffly, and knew she must be in shock. Micah joined him as he sidled a short distance from the small, seated figure. She looked helpless, just sitting there rocking and crying.

"We'll stay here for the night," Yago said quietly. He went to the girl and carefully placed the quilt around her shoulders.

The brothers discussed gathering firewood, which would be difficult to find now that darkness was falling and everything was wet. It took some time, but eventually they had enough wood to last until morning. Micah had found their horses in the hills just north of where the cabin had been. He hobbled them near the swollen river; then returned with bedrolls, some grub and dry lucifers.

Yago discovered the girl still sitting, staring into the evening gloom with wretched despair. He took her under the arms and gently pulled her to her feet. She walked in a trance, numbly, as he led her toward the campsite. He steered her down the steps into the cellar.

Separated from Micah and Yago by the fire, she looked at them with haunted eyes and refused to eat anything. They conferred in low, quiet tones as to what to do about her.

"We'll take her to the nearest settlement," Yago said. "This loss seems to have becrazed her."

Micah shook his head impatiently. "I say we bring her home with us. She doesn't appear to have any family. That vortex has stolen her whole life!"

Typical of Micah, Yago thought knowingly. Always so generous, so softhearted. Willing to take any stray under his wing.

"She's garbed in shabby men's clothing, Micah! She looks like that rough female scout we've heard about, Calamity Jane."

"Calamity Jane wouldn't be acting this way over any old homestead."

"Look, Micah, I'm not uncaring, I'm just tired . . . we can discuss this in the morning. Perhaps she'll have come to her senses by then."

* * *

Rebecca awoke at dawn before the two men did, and stealthily climbed the ladder without disturbing them. She wandered her property, carefully picking her way. She now had control of her reasoning and she didn't cry. She had to make plans if she were to survive.

To give up on the homestead was an unfathomable idea. It would be like discarding a living part of herself. Through many adversities, alone she'd learned to cope with the farm life. She'd endured an enormous blizzard last year, and the grasshopper invasion this year. Dreadful things, but she'd prevailed.

Rebecca came upon her mother's old steamer trunk, with one corner smashed in but the lid still secured. She unlatched it and rummaged through the contents, removing a pair of her father's duck-cloth pants and a flannel shirt. She found his battered slouch hat and pressed it to her nose, inhaling his scent.

"Oh, Papa! I miss you so."

She withdrew two more items from the trunk: a small, much-used Bible, and a coiled plaited-leather whip. She uncurled the whip and wrapped it around her petite waist, tucking the tip, the cracker, under the handle. She looked at the small book with moist eyes. Her mother had used it to teach her to read. They'd practiced penmanship and ciphering, too, during house-bound winter days.

Enough! Stop looking back and look forward instead. Be strong, be a woman of purpose.

But Rebecca's shoulders slumped. She knew she'd been defeated. She couldn't stay on the farm, for she lacked the physical prowess to rebuild. Nor had she the means to buy grain for the animals or other commodities for the long winter ahead. It had become obvious her life was to go in another direction. But where?

A rooster crowed sharply in raucous response to the morning light. Another thought pierced her heart: *What will I do with the animals? I can't just leave them to roam on their own.*

She thought of greedy, grabby Mr. Starns and shuddered. That miserly man coveted her land, and her body, too, if he could get his hands on her. She raised her brows as a thought struck her concerning the tightfisted man. *I could make a quick and easy sale to Starns. He'd take the hogs and chickens, too.*

She'd have to go to the claims office in Yankton and change the deed. Ennis, the land agent, had been a good friend to Father. He'd kindly watched out for Rebecca after her parents' passing. But the thought of going into town brought with it icy dread. Besides, how could she just give up and leave this place, abandoning the dream? Her folks hadn't raised her to be a quitter. After twenty minutes of difficult deliberation, she knew what she had to do. She'd made up her mind.

* * *

She knew one thing. She couldn't stay in Yankton. Rebecca's lip curled in disgust and her chin lifted stubbornly at the remembrance of the bright afternoon when a small delegation of old women from town had stopped by. They'd come shortly after her mother's burial.

"Young ladies have no business farming on their own," one of the do-gooders had pronounced aggressively. "They should be looking after a man and having children." They abhorred the fact that she refused to marry stuffy old Mr. Aarsen, who'd tried to court her. *I was only eighteen and he was older than my own father!*

Rebecca recalled the day last spring when Aarsen's sister had helped her make soap. She could almost smell the melted fat and hot lye water as she relived the moment. The elderly Miss Aarsen had meant well when she'd cautioned, in her quavery voice, that people branded Rebecca as an eccentric. Some of the people in and around Yankton frowned upon her, to be sure, perhaps more now than they had four years ago. Part of their problem was based on the clothes she wore.

Over time her own dresses had become threadbare and tattered, and then she'd worn her mother's to rags. Besides, men's clothes worked best for farming, she thought obstinately. *It really bothered the biddies when I wore my father's clothes to church!*

But Rebecca didn't care. The garments she wore to services may have been old and masculine, but they were clean and they were neatly pressed.

Stories about her spread like wildfire—townsfolk forgot the respect they once held for her family. As people overlooked the real Rebecca, she became more and more the recluse, dodging others as much as possible. And they, nudging and smirking, avoided her; some cast cold glances up and down her person when she trod the boardwalk.

"Obviously I cannot stay in Yankton," she said aloud. "I won't." Her meandering brought her back over a small knoll and she saw the two men. The dark one was the older of the two, she knew that for certain.

What did they call themselves? Yago and . . . was it Michael? No, that wasn't it.

She walked toward them and they motioned to her, coming forward to meet her. The blond boy abruptly asked, "We didn't get your name last night—what is it?" His words came out in a rush.

She smiled faintly. "I'm Rebecca. Rebecca LaRoche. And who did you say you were again?"

"Malachi Conrad, but Micah for short. Thanks for the shelter las—"

Yago broke in. "Can you tell us where exactly is the settlement of Yankton? We realize it must be somewhere near here. You see, we're looking for our older brother and last we heard from him, he was there."

"I have to attend to some business in town. If you'll wait some, I'll take you there today. What's your brother's name? Maybe I know him."

"Cooper Conrad," Yago answered.

Rebecca's heart leaped at the mention of his name. "Y—yes. I know him. I—I know where you can find him. He works at the mill in Yankton."

She scrutinized both the Conrads, looking for Cooper in their faces. Now she saw it, a family resemblance! Yago's dark locks of hair falling over his forehead, the beginnings of the same rakish grin in Micah. Rebecca noticed that Micah's eyes had roved to her shirt front. She peered down to see what it was that had him gaping. Her shirt was open halfway to her belly button. Her face radiated heat as she hastily corrected the problem.

No wonder he stared at me like I was a wanton hussy. Her skin glowed deep pink from embarrassment.

Yago spoke up. "If you'd kindly give us directions, I think my brother and I would make better time by ourselves."

"You know, my roof saved your hides last night and

you owe me one," asserted Rebecca. "I have to see a truly revolting man today by the name of Mr. Starns, and I would really like to have you with me when I speak to him."

"C'mon, Yago, what's the harm in another hour?" Micah said, coming to her aid.

"Fine," Yago said, making no effort to hide his annoyance.

Rebecca gathered her meager belongings upon her mother's quilts and rolled them into a bundle. She crushed her father's old felt hat down low on her head. Then she turned, narrowed her eyes, and scrutinized the ravaged land, seeing what it had been rather than the spoiled dream before her. Her eyes slid to a grassy patch and the rich beige coat of . . . *Madam! How can I leave that dear old girl behind?*

* * *

Yago made his regret quite evident. It clearly rankled him that they were taking Madam along with them. He'd stared incredulously and cursed under his breath when Rebecca had led the cow to where they waited. The boy, Micah, smiled shyly when he handed her the reins of one of the packhorses, the sorrel. The animal had been relieved of most of its load. "This is Buster," he said. "He's a fair ridin' horse."

They rode fast at first, but Madam, the poor beast, looked miserable as her big milkbag swung hideously from side to side. And so it was they walked.

They reached Yankton after the supper hour. With the quiet emptiness of the flatlands behind them, Rebecca felt the city fairly hum with activity. People congregated at the hotel and strolled along the wooden sidewalks.

Rebecca found the Starns house amongst a clutter of clapboard buildings.

Mr. Starns took obvious pleasure in the news of her misfortune and his own stroke of luck. He also seemed anxious, as though he feared that Rebecca might change her mind. He hustled all of them to the claims office, only to find that the agent, Ennis, had closed for the night. In what Rebecca knew to be a feverish state of avarice, Starns pressed her to walk with him the short distance to Ennis' house. Yago and Micah left her then, in search of their brother.

The rousted Ennis grasped the situation almost immediately. Hair tousled, collar loosened, he glanced at Rebecca repeatedly. His concern for her was apparent.

"Are you sure you want to do this?" he asked. "Don't you want to give it more thought?"

Rebecca placated her loyal friend, assuring him that she was certain. Finally Starns had the claim in his grasping hands, and Rebecca's pockets were heavy with gold slugs and coins.

Starns made his getaway, leaving the girl standing on the stoop, holding Madam's lead. Had Yago and Micah found their brother? A yearning coiled through her body, and wishful thoughts of Cooper filled her mind.

* * *

A mill worker told the Conrad boys that Cooper's workday had ended and they might find him at one of the saloons. Several such boisterous establishments sat along the riverfront. The brothers tied their horses to a hitching post before searching first one saloon, then another. In each dim interior, the stink of stale beer and rank spittoons filled the air. They found Cooper in the third watering hole they tried. They immediately spotted his lanky frame sprawled in a chair, with a woman draped all over him.

There he sat, drinking a jigger of whiskey with one hand and embracing a beautiful woman with the other. The two of them were laughing and talking, heads together. Yago saw that her painted face was playful and Coop wore a wicked smile. The woman's low-cut bodice was molded to her body. "The better to display her buxom wares," Yago said out of the corner of his mouth.

He saw that Micah's wide eyes were fastened on the woman's chest. As the brothers neared the table, she noticed them before Cooper did.

"Well, what have we here?" she said, her tone inviting, her eyes burning into them. Cooper followed her gaze and, in one smooth motion, had the woman on her feet as he headed toward them.

"James! Malachi!" he exclaimed, hugging them to him. Then, with worry in his voice, "What are the two of you doing here?" The concerned tone told Yago that his older brother feared that which had brought them to him. A moment of silence followed as Yago wondered where he should start.

"Papa passed away five weeks ago. Mother sent us here to tell you to come home."

Cooper abruptly sat in the nearest chair. "I see," he finally said.

Yago saw turbulence in his eyes, a look of denial, then horror and deep, deep sorrow. Cooper shook his head slowly. "I should have been there," he whispered.

"It happened real fast—there was no way for you to know," Micah said, and then he told of the accident.

"Still, I should have let him know I loved him, even if we never could get along," Cooper said softly. "I realized some time ago he was just trying to look after me. I . . . I just bucked everything he tried to do for me." Grief made his deep voice husky.

"Part of it was his refusal to consider any of my

ideas for the ranch, for improving the herd, or . . ." He gazed into a void, remembering; then shook his head again. "So stubborn, and yet he allowed Mother to boss him around somethin' fierce. I should've let him know that at last I did understand, and that I loved him very much. I meant to, but I kept putting it off."

"Look, Coop," Yago said. "Papa is probably up there," he nodded heavenward, "looking down and saying the same things you are. Maybe there's some other way of making it right. You'll just have to find it."

A thick, gloomy silence hung between them for a moment until Micah broke it. "Will you come home?"

Yago put his earnest face close to Coop's. "We need you, with Papa gone. I don't have a head for business, and you were always so good at those matters."

Coop shook his head. "I don't know. This is so sudden. . . . I have a good position at the Flouring Mill. I don't want to up and leave the owner without a manager. We had plans to expand with more products, eastern markets. I'll have to give it some thought."

Yago felt apprehensive about his next task, the unpleasant duty of informing Cooper about the will and the pressing matter it entailed. He completed the chore with great effort, finishing with a flourish. "By July, 1876, you must be hitched, married! You'd be what, how old then? Twenty-five?"

The three of them sat through another round of glum silence, which Cooper punctuated with a heavy sigh.

"If I do go home, boys, I'd have to tie up some loose ends, but not tonight. Have the two of you had anything to eat lately? I stay at Ash's Hotel, and they serve the best catfish this side of the Missouri."

"I'm famished!" Micah said with unbridled enthusiasm. "Cooper, wait till you hear what we've been through."

Yago and Cooper laughed in unison as they followed Micah out of the barroom door. They nearly bumped into him when he stopped abruptly. The girl, Rebecca, stood near their tethered horses, hat in hand. She looked lost in the fading sunlight.

She still has that cow in tow, Yago thought, *and she seems so lonely and sad. Obviously she was waiting for us.*

Micah looked back at his brothers and nodded in her direction. "Suppose she's hungry too? Coop, Rebecca here saved our lives yesterday!"

The girl's eyes collided with Cooper's.

Chapter Three

Cooper's eyes fused with hers. Her unusual eyes—*so green!*— emphasized her cheeks, ruddy from the sun. Outdoor work had turned her skin lightly tawny. She was a bit of a thing, boyish in her masculine attire. Her rough shirt had been tucked into men's pants that were rolled up at the bottoms; a bullwhip encircled her waist, accentuating its smallness and the curve of her hip.

He couldn't simply dismiss her as the strange, uncultivated farm girl that people talked about so callously. He found himself looking more deeply into her oval face and those large, lustrous eyes.

"I—I just want to say how sorry I am about your father," she said softly. "Micah told me about it during our ride here today."

Cooper murmured a thank-you. He couldn't keep himself from staring at her generous mouth, her pale golden skin.

"Come have supper with us, Rebecca," Malachi said impetuously.

She shook her head at the boy. "I'm not hungry, but I appreciate the invite." She lowered her head and Cooper watched her shiny, sun-streaked crown disappear under the weather-beaten slouch hat.

"Come with us when we go home tomorrow," Malachi blurted out.

That impulsive boy and his tenderhearted disposition, thought Cooper. Yago rolled his eyes and exchanged looks with Cooper that said, *He'd do it, too. Drag her all the way back to our part of Wyoming Territory if we let him.*

"Thanks," Rebecca said, her face flushed, "but I'll have to think about that. Perhaps we should wait until tomorrow when we all have a better idea of what we want to do. I'm sure you want to discuss things between the three of you anyway."

"Good idea," Yago put in quickly.

Cooper suspected the girl had seen the reluctant look that had passed between Yago and himself. *It was ill-mannered of us*, he thought, feeling sheepish.

"Where will you go until then?" asked Malachi, obviously worried about her. "Where will we meet tomorrow?" The boy refused to back down, even when he saw Yago giving him eyes of warning.

Rebecca wouldn't look at Cooper. "There's a creek bed about two miles from town, to the west. It has two cottonwoods that form a 'V.' Your older brother probably knows where it is. You'll find me there."

Still Malachi wasn't finished. "Here, take Buster—just for tonight," he proffered.

Little brother was mighty thoughtful, thought Cooper as he nodded his head in assent. Yago mumbled his own agreement.

The slight figure of the girl turned and, leading the horse and cow, slowly walked away into the gathering dusk. She never looked back.

* * *

Coop couldn't remember a time when Malachi had

seemed more stubborn. The kid was wholeheartedly determined to take Rebecca with them.

"I don't want you to get your hopes up over this girl; she'll just end up hurting your feelings," Coop said as soon as they entered his hotel room. "Remember that snapping turtle you once rescued, Micah? The one the ranch hands were going to use for target practice? And we had to help you with it so you wouldn't get your finger bit off? The girl probably won't even show up tomorrow, because she has a place of her own. She'll just take the horse and go."

"I think I better clarify something here," Yago said. "She lost everything last night in a tornado. Her farmstead is leveled." Yago retold the story from the first signs of the thunderstorm up until they'd found Coop. "I think Micah just feels sorry for the girl. I do, too, in a way. You weren't there to see her after all that wind. It was pitiful."

"And she has no one!" Malachi sputtered.

"I see," Cooper said. "That throws a different light on the matter. But she's wild! They call her Dakota Reb, and that's not short for Rebecca. You haven't heard the things about her that I have. She is just rebellious about everything. That's where the nickname comes from, 'Dakota Rebel.'"

Yago added his arguments to Cooper's. "And what would Mother think if we dragged home an uncivilized nester. A *squatter*?"

"Ma's been wanting to add to the house staff," Malachi retorted. "She'd like to have another domestic!"

Cooper felt frayed, uncomfortable. "Dakota Reb is different. Unusual. I doubt she'd be docile enough to be a housekeeper."

"I say we give her a chance, at least," Malachi bargained, "and I'll tell Ma that, too!"

"What about the damned cow?" Yago muttered,

frowning. "She won't leave it. It seems like that one thing, that blasted cow, means everything to her. We couldn't get her to go without it." He shook his head. "It would be like taking a beloved puppy away from a little boy who just lost his whole world."

Cooper understood his brother's tone. Yago had tried to sound brusque, but under the irritation Cooper heard a sensitive and empathetic person.

Malachi leaned forward. "Look, I know it'll take us a little longer with the cow along, and Ma will fuss and worry if we don't get back timely-like. But—"

"Fine," Cooper relinquished. "If she goes along, the trip will take us three or four weeks instead of two, but remember, Malachi, Reb is your responsibility."

"Oh, so you've decided to come home with us?" Yago asked with obvious relief.

Coop was taken by surprise. He had missed his family, and he did feel responsible about the ranch. A search of his heart told him it wasn't the inheritance that drew him back home . . . it was his duty to care for the clan.

"Yes, of course," he said.

Throughout the remainder of the evening, Coop felt uneasy. He had misgivings about the intractable girl. He couldn't seem to forget some of the townspeople's derision of her. The way she'd come to church in the past! It just wasn't right. Yet, he wondered: Where was she? Was she all right? Would she be at the meeting place tomorrow?

* * *

She had to meet them tomorrow, Rebecca knew, to return their horse if nothing else. What to do now? Where to go? Her stomach still flip-flopped from being so near to Cooper, talking to him. The sight of him outside the saloon had made her tongue-tied. She hadn't even said his name! He looked so appealing, with his broad chest and his narrow hips and his well-muscled thighs.

She'd seen the reluctant glance that had passed between the two older brothers; she'd surmised they were not keen on her going with them tomorrow. Cooper's stare had made her painfully aware of her appearance, from unbound hair to worn work-shoes. He was accustomed to a fine dress on a woman, fancy shoes, and a bonnet. Her cheeks burned with mortification—he'd heard the whispers in Yankton! She knew what he must think of her and it made her heart hurt.

Suddenly the horse tugged the reins, dipping his head to tear off a clump of grass alongside the road. Rebecca had walked the animals to the edge of town without realizing it. She leaned over and whispered into Madam's soft fawn ear, "Let's get out of here, old girl. Are you up to it?"

* * *

Rebecca made camp a mile from the point she'd said she would meet the Conrad men. After she settled into her bedroll, she stared into the blackness and the stars that seemed to march on forever. Her mind stewed with disquietude.

How could I have given up the homestead so easily? How could I abandon my parents' dream?

She swallowed hard and told herself that, although her life had been turned upside down, she would make a new one. If she had to, she'd start over. Have a home to call her own. With or without a man.

Rebecca awoke early, hungry, and she hadn't slept well. The day was still, clear and warm. She had hours to wait. May as well move into the shade. She put dirt on her dead fire and moved her bedroll farther under the bushes. She crawled in and dozed to the sound of chirping birds.

The wagon's moving too fast for the corner—I can feel it tipping! The horses are stumbling as the wagon tongue pulls at them. The ground is rushing up to meet my face!

Rebecca jerked awake, breathing heavily. "A dream," she said aloud. "Just a dream." But still she heard the creaking of wagon wheels and the clopping of a horse's hooves. She crawled forward quietly to peer through the shrubbery.

A buggy with two people aboard stopped along the trail. Rebecca's eyes were drawn to the bright blond, wavy hair of the passenger. A woman. Liza Wright. Rebecca studied the beautiful girl as if she were a grand painting. That crop of brilliant hair setting off her other perfect features. She was rich. She wore elegant clothes. The stunning Liza. She had been blessed with good luck.

Madam and the horse, Buster, were out of sight but within earshot. Rebecca hoped fervently they wouldn't give away her hiding place. Her gaze shifted to see who accompanied the pretty girl. "It's Cooper!" she whispered. Her heart sank. His long legs, snug in tight dark pants and high black boots, were folded into the carriage next to Liza's. The immaculate white shirt he wore set off his dark good looks to full advantage.

The couple began to kiss and hug. It pained her to watch, but Rebecca couldn't drag her eyes away. She heard them murmuring to one another between caresses.

"When will I see you again?" Liza asked plaintively. She arranged her lovely face into a pout. Cooper mumbled a response in an undertone too low for Rebecca to understand. Liza began to cry.

Rebecca's heart pounded and her ears rang with jealousy. *He's a rake and a rounder and he'll never be mine! How could he possibly see anything but rubbish in me after being with someone as flawless as Liza?*

Then she took a deep breath and squared her shoulders as if preparing to do battle. *Don't dwell on him! Forget him. Anything would be better than feeling like this!*

To Rebecca it was an eternity before Cooper urged the carriage horse onward. When the conveyance finally pulled away, she exhaled with a soft moan, feeling as if she'd held her breath the whole time. She pressed her hand to her speeding heart, thankful that her presence in the bushes had not been revealed.

Rebecca's stomach grumbled; she prowled along the creek bed until a grazing rabbit caught her eye. She eased her whip from her waist and propelled it deftly, wrapping the tip around the rabbit's neck. With a flick she broke it quickly, mercifully.

No time to skin and roast it, she thought. She'd get to the meeting place and would eat there. She saddled Buster and prepared to leave. With the rabbit tied onto the saddle and Madam's lead in hand, she rode to the rendezvous point to wait.

At the two cottonwoods that formed a "V" Rebecca staked the animals and gathered wood for a fire. Now she could cook dinner and fill her empty, complaining stomach. From across the still prairie, though, she heard the distant sounds of horses and men.

"Yo! Dakota Reb! Are you there?" She recognized Micah's voice.

Rebecca stiffened with resentment upon hearing that horrible nickname. She knew Cooper must have opposed her going with them—surely he'd filled their heads with scorn and contempt for her. Obviously Yago felt disinclined to have her go along, even before he heard about "Dakota Rebel." *I can't make a fresh start with that reputation following me.*

Rebecca emerged from her crouch, her mouth stubbornly mute with anger. She'd made her decision.

"There you are," Micah said with a genuine smile on his face.

The Conrad brothers, mounted, stared down at her. She felt the magnetic pull of Cooper's eyes on hers and she resisted. She struggled with herself to keep very still, refusing to allow her features or her body language to betray her roiling emotions.

"Thanks for loaning Buster to me—I'll get him for you," she said, forcing herself to speak evenly.

"Aw, no, Reb, you gotta come along!" Micah wheedled.

"No, I don't want to inconvenience you three." She risked a glare at Cooper. The suction of his gaze pulled her in; she struggled to look away. "Madam and I would slow you down far too much. It would be a great imposition."

Then she heard what she hadn't expected: Cooper and Yago chiming in with their little brother, urging her to change her mind! But they didn't really mean it, she thought. They were just trying to be polite.

"Ahem," Yago cleared his throat. "Our mother could use more help in the house, if you're interested. Daisy is our only domestic, and—"

Cooper interrupted. "Can you do anything besides farm work?" His tone was light and teasing.

She drew herself up, eyes flashing. *He's mocking me! Can I do anything besides—what gall!*

But Yago's suggestion, his offer, had been very kind. Perhaps the middle brother had sympathy for her plight after all, and for that she felt grateful.

Cooper's eyes glinted darkly. He used the bantering tone again. "Now, boys, I suppose Rebel's thinking there's something not quite proper about a young woman traveling alone with three men for such an extended period." A glimmer of deviltry crossed his handsome face.

And there it was. The same rogue's grin, the

seductive smile he flashed at every female! Her mixed feelings were tearing her apart. Anger. Longing. Distress. Need.

The cloudless day had turned hot and airless. Cooper's rugged chin still pointed her way, his sly smile contrasting whitely with his tanned face. Rebecca's skin flamed hot and damp.

Cooper hadn't finished with his needling. "Perhaps we could persuade the young lady to ride with us if we trade in a pack saddle for a sidesaddle."

"Not for me, you won't!" Rebecca had drawn herself into a proud posture. "I'll go astride or on foot, but I won't ride all crooked and lopsided!"

He beamed triumphantly. "Then you'll go. Let's be on our way soon, then."

Rebecca, still feeling peppery, swore to herself she wouldn't allow Cooper Conrad to trifle with her. *I am going with them, though. I do believe he bedeviled me into it.*

Mica grinned widely at her, with a look of relief in his eyes, and then he pointed to the dead rabbit. "Haven't you eaten anything yet, Reb?"

"I'll wait, she said as she gathered Madam's lead rope. She climbed into Buster's saddle and added, "I don't want to waste any more time."

Yago began to rummage around in his saddlebag. "Here," he said, "some jerked venison. Gnaw on that to keep the hunger down until we stop again."

Cooper urged his horse forward. "Are we ready, then?"

Chapter Four

Cooper felt curious about this Rebel, this Rebecca LaRoche, but he didn't harbor the pity for her that his brothers seemed to have. Micah and Yago hadn't heard the rumors. They didn't realize she probably was as self-sufficient as any man. She didn't *need* their protection.

Yet, today his eyes had been irresistibly drawn to hers, just as they'd been the evening before, and had lingered over her smooth, sun-kissed skin. Even clothed in a homemade man's shirt and heavy pants, her trim, fine-boned body looked good. She moved elegantly, gracefully.

They plodded onward in the heat-soaked landscape, the cow bringing up the rear. A hawk floated on the current high in the clear turquoise sky. More thoughts of the girl washed into Cooper's mind.

An unwelcome notion intruded: Micah seemed to be infatuated with the girl, but he was only sixteen. Their mother would be nettled, indeed. *She'll be fit to be tied.*

Cooper stared blankly at the bleached-out hills in the distance as speculation about the girl continued to plague him.

The heat of the day finally lessened in the early

evening, but they rode on until twilight. Alongside a creek, a flock of white cranes made a slow, undulating departure. Micah saw to the horses while Rebel cared for the cow. Cooper watched her tender ministrations, heard her murmurings to the animal while he and Yago made camp. He found it hard to imagine her speaking so tenderly to a child . . . or to a man.

All three of the brothers kneeled to prepare a fire and their supper. Micah was twisting dried grasses when Rebel spoke from behind: "Is it all right with you gentlemen if I avail myself of the river first?"

They nodded, averted their eyes and studiously turned their backs to the creek.

"Wait!" Cooper said. He found a small, paper-wrapped cube of soap and gave it to her.

"Thanks," she said.

* * *

No teasing about a dirty dirt farmer. I'm surprised he didn't take that opportunity to beleaguer me, Rebecca thought in amazement. He'd comported himself far better than she'd imagined he would. She'd sensed that Cooper, much more than Yago, resented poor Madam and her big milk bag slowing their progress.

It would feel so good to be clean again! She couldn't wait to wash her hair and rinse out her shirt, socks, her underthings. She glanced back—no one was looking—but she walked around an outcropping and out of sight anyway.

The next morning, inexplicably, Rebecca felt relaxed and tranquil for the first time in many days; in her positive mood she relished the breezy and temperate weather. Nothing could ruin her disposition today, not even Cooper's testiness or his sullen stare at the dear dawdler, Madam.

Micah pulled in his horse beside hers. His blond

head was hatless, his hair windblown. The impish grin spreading across his face reminded her of Coop's. "Buster's trot is awful uncomfortable, isn't it, Reb?"

The big sorrel did have a choppy gait, but Rebecca didn't mind. They rode on in companionable silence, gazing at the sea of tall grass prairie. The scattered homesteads were fewer now. Soon they would disappear altogether.

"Tell me about yourself, Reb. Do you have any kinfolk who could've helped you with your farm?" Micah asked. "I know it was hard for you to give it up."

Rebecca stretched in her saddle, an innocent yet catlike movement, and began to talk. She told the boy about her parents and all she'd learned from them. They'd been wonderful teachers. Besides book learning, her mother had taught her the womanly arts: cooking, canning, embroidery, quilting, tatting, and mending. She'd learned how to process meat and cure hides. Her father, half Lakota, had been a teamster, a bullwhacker.

"Wait—you're part Indian?" Yago spoke up, an entranced look on his face. Rebecca hadn't been aware that he'd eased his horse near theirs.

"He taught me the Lakota language," she said proudly. "We spent much time outdoors together. From him I learned animal husbandry and hunting. Before he settled down with my mother, he'd driven oxen or mules for settlers from the east." Rebecca chuckled. "Mother always laughed about the fiendish swearing—she said teamsters used oaths of the blackest kind. But he gave that up when he met my mother."

Then Rebecca told them of her parents' accident. "It was four years ago. They'd gone into Yankton to sell grain. I'd wanted to go along." *To catch a glimpse of Cooper at the mill,* she thought poignantly.

"My folks and I planned to go to town together,

but, before leaving, Father looked after the animals and found a gilt just beginning to farrow her first litter of piglets. I had to stay home to look after the gilt." Rebecca stared ahead, eyes fixed in the past. "The pig did fine, but Papa and Mama didn't."

Don't relive that terrible time, she admonished herself, but the pictures were running through her head and she couldn't stop them.

"Papa had just purchased a matched pair of Belgians three days before. The horse trader, Mr. Shay, had sworn they were well-broke, but they spooked on the way into town. They ran wildly out of control until the buckboard overturned." She shuddered; then went on. "The team must've been very green—otherwise Papa could've handled them."

Her voice was soft now. "The impact crushed both my parents. Papa died instantly, but Mama endured in pain for several days, everyone helpless to mend her. The horses were unharmed. From the looks of him, Mr. Shay was ashamed to his very soul." She recalled how abject he'd looked, head down, leading the team away. "He refunded the purchase price," she said with a humorless smile.

"Some of the womenfolk from town gave what comfort and aid they could, but I spent an awful three days at my mother's side."

"Be strong," her mother had whispered from her deathbed. *"Be a woman of purpose." I've tried, Mama. I really have.*

"I still miss my folks every day, just as you must miss your father," she finished.

Micah and Yago had listened in apparent fascination. The youngest boy wore an expression of admiration.

Cooper frowned and threw the trio a glance that revealed his irritation. Rebecca nearly sniggered, enjoying her connection to Coop's brothers. Enjoying the fact that she, for once, annoyed him rather than the other way around.

They camped that night in a sparsely wooded area thick with prairie chickens. The birds made a delicious supper, accompanied by Madam's milk, hard bread, coffee, and dried plums Rebecca had stewed over the fire.

Stomach satisfied, Rebecca sat a distance from the men, idly toying with her bullwhip. She uncoiled and coiled it again with speed and dexterity.

"Reb's papa was a muleskinner, Coop," Micah said. "He trained her how to use that thing. Isn't that right, Reb?"

She nodded. "He told me 'A young girl out here on the prairie needs ways to protect herself.' He taught me how to let the whip become an extension of my own hand," she said, flipping her wrist. "He taught me how to allow the whip to do the work. The whip always does exactly what you tell it to do. If you're impatient," she glanced at Cooper, "the whip will give you a painful reminder to modify your behavior."

Coop glowered at them and said nothing.

* * *

Three days later they crossed the Missouri.

They'd passed through a desolate ocean of billowing grass, beaten by the wind. They'd seen a slew of deer each morning and evening, and at night they'd heard the plaintive yelping of coyotes. Tall, lush vegetation had given way to scantier, shorter grass on the gentle, undulating hills. The river, wide and slow, glinted in the late July sun. Waterfowl glided on its surface; in places, cottonwood trees clung to its banks.

That night, from the other side of the fire, Cooper made his way to where Rebecca sat. He loomed over her, intense. She thought the dark stubble that shadowed his firm jaw only made him more tempting.

"I figured I'd point out to you, Rebel, that we're in rattler country now. They like to crawl into bedrolls at night when it's cool."

Rebecca nodded her understanding. He turned and walked away, and she said softly, "You expect me to sleep, knowing that?"

Yago heard and chuckled.

* * *

The chill of the early morning would soon melt away in the strong sunshine. Cooper and the boys had quietly risen and begun preparing for another day on the trail. The girl, however, remained wrapped tightly in her blankets, motionless. Suddenly apprehensive, Cooper went to her and gently touched her shoulder.

She stirred, sending a wave of relief through him.

"I'm-m 'wake," she slurred drowsily. She sat up and languorously flexed in a feline stretch.

Cooper didn't think, then, about how stubborn she'd been to bring that damnable cow. He didn't think about others' opinion of her back in Yankton. He didn't think about anything except her veil of shining hair, glowing red-gold around the edges with the rising sun behind it. And her rosy cheeks and lips, soft and full, as she smiled sleepily.

"Time's wastin'." Cooper's voice sounded gruff even to himself. He knew he'd been cross and touchy lately . . . and with good reason. The four of them were trespassers in Indian territory. They were in danger there, and the sooner they reached home the better.

"Cinch up soon—we must go," Cooper ordered brusquely.

* * *

The cow slogged along behind them in the shimmering heat haze; Cooper's scowl deepened with each dragging mile. They passed a ranging prairie dog town and, later, a meadow filled with white and yellow wildflowers. Cooper scanned the vista ceaselessly. He spotted a small dark cluster in the distance, and pointed it out to the others. "Buffalo," he said, "bison, a pitifully small herd. Just a few years ago, there would've been a gigantic black mass of a herd as far as the eye could see, instead of a pathetic bunch like this."

Thoughts of decimation of the buffalo saddened Cooper, and the scorching, dusty day did nothing to improve his morale. The hot, constant wind tore at them. It scoured their faces and lashed their hair.

I feel like a fool, he brooded, *letting that blamed girl lasso us into this, holding us down. But as untoward as she is, she does intrigue me somehow.*

He thought her tribal nose, with its strong bridge, suited her face perfectly. Her eyes changed color sometimes, from sea-green to jade to—

Rebecca maneuvered Buster alongside, interrupting his thoughts. "I want you to know how much I appreciate what you and your brothers are doing for me," she said solemnly. "I'm grateful."

Cooper presented her with his easy grin. His irritable mood had vanished like the buffalo. His mind told his restless heart that Rebel—Rebecca—would be an easy conquest, another notch on his belt.

* * *

When it happened, they were camped near the gnarled terrain of *mako sica*, the badlands. The night had been cold, the fire smoky. Rebecca awoke and saw that the two younger Conrads had started breakfast.

Usually Cooper was the one to rise first, but today he still slept.

This is my chance to milk Madam before he can start complaining about her, Rebecca thought. She stealthily stepped past Cooper, and then she heard it—a buzzing sound, the tell-tale rattle. A cold spurt of fear shot through her. She saw sweat on Cooper's brow. Her green eyes found his terrified brown ones and locked there.

Zuzuecha! she thought, paralyzed. She called softly to Yago. "Snake! There's a snake in with Cooper. I'm afraid if I move, it'll bite him."

Yago froze, eyes wide. Micah hadn't heard the warning.

The boy came walking swiftly toward Cooper's bed roll, unsuspecting. "Come on, lazy, get up! What's gotten into you this morning?"

"Micah!" hollered Yago. "It's a rattler!"

Micah stopped in his tracks, color draining from his face. His footsteps had set off the rattling again, louder this time.

Rebecca swallowed. *How long can Cooper endure it without moving?*

Micah pulled his gun out of its holster.

"We can't shoot it!" said Yago as he slowly crept forward. "We might hit Coop."

"I have an idea," Rebecca whispered, holding Cooper's frightened eyes with hers. She carefully sidestepped to her pack of belongings. "Blink once for no and twice for yes."

"I hope you know what you're doing," Yago said from behind her.

Rebecca's eyes remained fastened on Cooper. "Do you understand?"

Cooper blinked twice.

"Is the snake near your upper chest, your neck?"

He blinked once.

"Is it beside your belly?"

One blink.

"Is it near your thigh?"

Cooper blinked twice.

Rebecca took a deep breath, found her whip and began to unwind it.

"What do you think you're doing?" asked Yago doubtfully. He put his hand on Rebecca's arm to stop her.

She ignored him and continued to speak to Cooper, "Do you trust me to do this?"

Cooper blinked twice. Rebecca raised her chin slightly in silent acknowledgment and transferred her eyes to Micah. She whispered, "When I nod, you pull that blanket off *fast*." She held her breath as Micah carefully knelt down and readied his hand to grab the blanket. Rebecca riveted Cooper again with steady eyes. "When he does that, you roll away." Rebecca looked at Micah, positioned her whip, and nodded.

Micah flipped off the blanket; Cooper rolled at the same time. The flat, broad head of the rattler raised to strike, its forked tongue flicking in and out. Rebecca's whip slithered through the air, seeking the triangular-shaped head. Within a second she'd severed the head from its wriggling body.

"Oh, God!" exclaimed Yago, wiping his damp forehead with a quivering hand. Malachi stayed kneeling on his heels, white and trembling, still clutching the blanket.

Cooper got to his feet shakily. He stepped forward and cupped Rebecca's hand in both of his. "I owe you my life."

She stared into his face and tried to swallow the lump in her throat. She couldn't speak. Cooper seemed reluctant to release her icy hand, but at last he did. She gathered the whip around her waist, looked back at the still-writhing body of the snake and shuddered.

Cooper hoisted the snake's light brown-green body and studied the distinctive markings, the yellowish belly. He counted the rattles. "Eight segments!" he announced. "And forty inches long, I'd say. A big one." He tossed it into the brush.

Yago shifted the snake's head with the toe of his boot. He seemed fascinated by its elliptical, cat-like eyes.

Micah watched all of them, his mouth still gaping in awe.

Cooper chuckled at his brothers. "Now you know why she's called Dakota Reb. She's no front-parlor miss."

"I'd better get Madam milked," Rebecca said quietly, and turned to go.

Behind her, she heard Yago speak teasingly to his older brother. "That ol' snake was probably a girl snake, Coop. She just wanted to cozy up to you like all the girls do."

"Not funny, James," Cooper replied.

* * *

Rebecca trailed the others. They were in the hills, slow going for the milk cow. Madam wasn't accustomed to thick underbrush, forest, and unlevel ground. Rebecca almost preferred the peace and quiet. *Lagging behind, at least I don't have to listen to his grumbling. He's making it easy for me to forget my infatuation for him.*

That's all it was, she told herself, *infatuation.*

"We're almost home, that's why Cooper's so impatient about Madam," Micah said, breaking into her thoughts.

The days had melted together until Rebecca had lost count. Was this the nineteenth day of their trek? The twentieth?

As if Micah felt the need to justify a big brother's failings, or to smooth things over, he continued: "He really isn't a bad guy. He's just worried about our safety. Can you forgive him?"

"I'm not angry with him, Micah. I just don't think I like him very much," Rebecca said with a dry, flat tone.

"Oh, all the girls love Coop," the boy stated confidently.

"He's a horse that's badly bridled," she said.

"You know, Reb, you're a very accomplished person. You're really capable with everything you do, but at the same time you aren't boastful or haughty about it. I like that. I like that a lot, Reb."

Rebecca blushed with the compliments. She felt the warmth crawl up her neck to her ears. "I don't know what to say."

"I think you and I can be good friends." Micah's golden-hazel eyes shone with innocent affection.

"Good friends," repeated Rebecca, almost to herself. "I think I'd like having a friend very much."

Chapter Five

Wyoming Territory

"This is desert country! Except for a thin, pitiful stream now and then, it's so very dry here," Rebecca exclaimed.

Yago reined his horse next to hers and mumbled, "Wyoming Territory isn't all like this. Our ranch is within the foothills of the Bearlodge Mountains, with a river flowing through it, and tall pine trees. . . . There's a tradin' post only about five miles from us." His unremarkable, honest face held a pensive expression.

"Rebecca, there's something I've been wanting to warn you about. Our mother is a rather, ahh, *formidable* woman. She's just as strong-willed as my brothers." Yago laughed and added, "I might even say she's as pigheaded as you!"

Rebecca smiled at the brawny young man, nodding her understanding. She changed the subject. "'Yago' . . . I've never known anyone by that name before."

"The Anglo is James. Call me James if you prefer."

"Oh, yes, I've heard Cooper use that once or twice. Did you know the James River is also called the Jacques? But I like 'Yago' for you." She added, as if to herself, "They call the James the Dakota River, too." She thought somberly of home. Then she said, "My last name, LaRoche, is French. It means 'the rock.'"

* * *

They saw many antelope as they rode—pronghorns, flashing their silvery sides and turning their white tails to them before springing away, bouncing and bobbing. The group also encountered an occasional herd of elk; they even witnessed a moose placidly grazing as they passed by. Sagebrush clumped the grayish-tan landscape. The sky, also gray, seemed as bleak and gloomy as Rebecca herself. Her lighthearted outlook had vanished along with the sun.

She mulled over Yago's words about his mother. Doubt and uncertainty rolled over her, buried her in misery. How could she have given up the land, betrayed her parents' memories like that? But she knew exactly how. *To follow Coop like a lovesick puppy,* she thought, disgusted with herself. Many nights on the trail, with him so near, she'd found it hard to sleep.

It would be mighty challenging to become a menial for the likes of Mrs. Conrad, it seemed. *It's far too late for second thoughts now,* she chided herself. But Rebecca swore that, no matter who she had to deal with, she would stay true to herself. She wouldn't—she *couldn't*—make herself into something she wasn't. She set her jaw and made a promise. *I resolve to create a new life for myself, somehow, a good life . . . and surely some land to call my own again. Someday.*

* * *

Cooper sat up from his bedroll just in time to see, fleetingly, a pair of staring foxes—mates, surely—not five yards away. Their coats shimmered silver-blue in the moonlight. Instantly, silently, they disappeared.

He glanced at the others. All asleep. Rebecca was curled into a ball of warmth in her bedding, her silken hair escaping the covers.

She's so much more than I expected, he mused. *Intelligent, and so capable, so expert with that bullwhip. Why, she could geld someone with that weapon!* It was enough to unnerve a man.

Cooper huddled under his blankets. He contemplated the way other women fawned over him, flirting with him, and the ways Rebecca differed from them. He heaved a great, troubled sigh.

I'll never allow myself to be emasculated, led around by the nose like that cow of hers, he told himself vehemently. *The girl is just another flower ripe for picking, and I'll be happy to oblige.*

* * *

The following evening the group came to a hill overlooking a large basin. Tall, flowing prairie grasses covered the valley floor that stretched before them for several miles. It reminded Rebecca of home. In the red glow of the setting sun, she discerned a well-worn trail that showed considerable use by buggies and wagons. They followed the thoroughfare to a fork in the road and stopped before a portal, a huge crossbar supported on each side by a tall post. It was marked with a brand, a lazy D inside the letter C.

The Conrad men were home.

"Hooee!" Cooper whooped, throwing his hat into the air and deftly catching it. He urged his horse into a flat-out gallop, leaving the others behind.

Rebecca noted that grassland extended into a rise of land covered with spruce and juniper. White-faced cattle dotted the area. She had never seen so many of the same breed in one place before. She rode along quietly, letting the boys' talk drift over her.

When they came around a bend sheltered by pine trees, she couldn't believe her eyes. To the west were several huge barns, corrals, granaries, smaller sheds and a long, narrow bunkhouse. She saw neat wooden fences around some of the smaller buildings. "This is remarkable! Back home even the richest folks don't have anything like this," she told no one in particular. Her voice had been drowned out by the joyous barking of a large wolf-like dog.

Cooper had dismounted; he stood amongst a small group of exhilarated, back-slapping cowboys. Rebecca swallowed with sudden nervousness and wished the earth would open up and take her.

A grizzled, gray-haired man joined the gathering. "Coop, boy! You're back!" exclaimed the older man. The two of them embraced.

"That's Chester," Micah said, pointing to the bent figure of the old man. "He's been here since before I was born." The boy jumped from his horse to greet the boisterous dog, who began lapping his face. "Duke! Did you miss me?"

More men approached to see what the commotion was all about. Rebecca couldn't help but smile with all the talking and elation and relief floating around her. She felt happy for Cooper and began to relax.

Madam and I aren't even noticed, she thought thankfully. She self-consciously touched her hair; she'd plaited it in the early morning, and wisps had escaped the braids during the long day.

"What's this? A sick moose?" The loud voice had an unpleasant tone.

Rebecca's head flew around to look over her shoulder. Behind her stood a tall, fair-haired man, legs spread in a gunslinger's stance. His arms were akimbo, hands on hips. He eyed Madam—and Rebecca herself—with a curious contempt.

"Don't you know that ugly thing can bring in diseases? We raise purebred Herefords here," he bellowed. Everyone focused on him.

The belligerent man worked his mouth and then spit a blackish-brown stream of chewing tobacco juice. Madam stood placidly chewing her cud. Her large deer-like ears didn't twitch as the man's disgusting saliva hit her round belly. Only the shiver of her skin and a darkening stain on her cream-colored hide gave evidence it had struck her.

He puffed up his chest and continued to spout off. "That thing is downright ugly! It'd be better off dead."

Rebecca undid the whip from her waist. No one noticed; they were watching the man with the big mouth, and the cow that had his attention. Another stream of tobacco spittle followed the first one.

"What say we shoot—"

Rebecca's whip uncoiled itself in front of his face with a snap. "She happens to be my animal, whom I hold in high esteem. If you can't control your mouth about her, I'll shut it for you," she said with command in her voice.

A fire sparked in her green eyes. She stared at the raw-boned man until his eyes shifted away. His jaw continued to work on the wad of tobacco; she positioned her hand for another strike.

"Reb!" Cooper shouted, arresting her wrist. The man spit his wad between his own two feet.

"Yago, who is he?" Cooper asked, jerking his head in the light-haired man's direction.

"That's Norman Kearn; he's the foreman Papa hired about three years ago," Yago said.

"You leave the girl and her cow alone," Cooper ordered quietly, through clenched teeth. "You hear me?"

Kearn bowed his head to Cooper, gave Rebecca a baleful sidelong glance, and fell back to the rear of the group.

"Break it up, men," Yago said, and laughed. "I'm sure Mother and Chalina are anxious to see our lost lamb." That brought a few guffaws from the crowd and they began to disperse. Many pairs of eyes swiveled covertly toward Rebecca as the men slowly took their leave.

Chester called to Coop as he strode away. "Yer Ma's got company tonight, boy. People stayin' over."

On foot, the small wayfaring troupe rounded another bend in the tree-lined lane. Suddenly the ranch house came into view.

Rebecca's breath caught at the sight of the huge home. A two-story log building of grand proportions stood there, surrounded by a railed, covered porch. A small enclosed yard, with a gate, sat in front of the house. At the rear, partially in view, a single-story addition gave the fine dwelling balance, made it even more impressive.

A picture of her little soddy passed quickly through Rebecca's mind, making her homesick for that which was forever gone. A new way of life now beckoned her.

Look at all that space. What do they do with it all?

Cooper's voice broke into her reverie. "Too bad there are other visitors here this evening."

"Yeah, we best go 'round the back, as grubby as we are," Yago said. "It would've been better if we'd had some private time to speak with Mother, instead of just springing Rebel on her in front of her guests."

"Right," replied Cooper slowly. He seemed to be deliberating. "Reb, would you mind sleeping in the barn—the hayloft—just for tonight? I know it doesn't seem very hospitable of me to ask, but . . ."

Rebecca nodded knowingly.

"C'mon, Reb, I'll show you," Micah said. Yago stood with his older brother, watching the slow-moving pair, with horse and cow, walk toward the stables in the failing evening light.

* * *

"Your cow should be right at home in here," Micah said as they entered the large, dim stable, leading Madam and Buster.

Rebecca breathed in the not-unpleasant aroma of animals and hay and leather. She aptly stripped the saddle and blanket from the sorrel. When she saw Micah reach for a horse brush, she turned to him and gently placed her hand on his arm.

"I can rub the horse down," she offered. "I know you must be anxious to get to your family."

"Thanks, Reb. You'll be safe up there," he said, his gaze lifting to the hayloft. "Don't worry about tomorrow. I'll make Mom understand."

"Hurry up, Micah!" Cooper barked from the entrance. "We'll all go around to the back and through the kitchen door together. Yago thinks it would be best if we clean ourselves up in our rooms first, before we see Ma and her guests."

Yago stood beside him. "G'night, Reb," he said gently.

Rebecca didn't watch the brothers leave, but went right to work making Buster comfortable.

"Howdy," said a cracked voice directly behind her, startling her. "Didn't mean ta skeer ya. The name's Chester. I see they got ya busy doin' my work, eh?"

"I asked to do it," replied Rebecca, "I wanted to make myself useful."

"Don't want ya up at the big house, eh?"

"Something like that," Rebecca said. She didn't trust the old man, although his watery blue eyes twinkled, and laugh lines were deeply etched around them. His smile was broad under a bristly gray moustache.

"Didn't think the Missus would go for the likes o'

you. She's a real feminine lady, and her daughter, too. Wouldn't take too kindly to a gal dressed in men's garb—especially one with them men-type manners you was sportin' out there." He tossed his head in the direction of the yard, and continued. "Called ya Reb, eh? What kinda name is that for a gal?"

"My name is Rebecca," she said with dignity and a touch of steam.

"Humph!" rumbled Chester. "That may be, but Reb fits the likes o' you better."

Rebecca stared at him with displeasure.

"Now, don't go gettin' your feathers ruffled. The truth is the truth and you should accept it as such."

"I can be just as much a lady as any of them in that big house," Rebecca protested.

"That may be. But you got a lot of boy in ya, too. And that's somethin' they ain't got," Chester said with certainty. "I don't know which one o' them boys took a fancy to ya, but their mama ain't gonna like it none. 'Specially if it was Coop." He added, as an afterthought, "More'n likely it was Coop." With more spirit, he said, "Ya mark my word, gal." He pointed a crooked finger at her. "The best thing for ya is to be movin' on. That boy's mama has plans for him!"

"I haven't come to be one of those boys' lightskirts. I came here to work as a maid," Rebecca said, feeling indignant.

"That as may be," Chester said. "I was told ya was ta bed down in the loft." He limped to a closed door that led to a tack room, and motioned for Rebecca to follow him. "Here be blankets. It gets mighty cold at night hereabouts." He handed several wool blankets to Rebecca. "Since ya be liken to do my job, I'll show ya where the water and feed be."

He led her to another door and opened it. Rebecca saw a grain bin and hay for the livestock. Chester took a pail from where they hung on pegs. "The water's out back," he said with a directional nod, and began to step past the stall where Madam shuffled softly about. He stopped momentarily to gaze at the camel-colored animal, shook his head, and clicked his tongue through his teeth. "What'd be the beast called?"

"Her name is Madam and she is a purebred Brown Swiss milk cow," Rebecca said with pride.

"Don't know as ta what purpose it'd be on this ranch." With a gnarled hand he rubbed the white stubble on his chin.

"You just wait until you eat her nice creamy butter on your batter cakes, and have her milk and cream in your soups."

"That as may be."

They continued to the watering trough. Chester took his leave after a few more instructions, and Rebecca relaxed. She saw to the animals' needs, happy to be working with the sweet creatures in the tranquil atmosphere of the quiet barn.

Her peaceful well-being vanished when she heard someone approach. Chester reappeared, carrying a tin plate covered with a flour-sack dish towel.

"Figgured ya had no supper, so Blackie—he cooks for the hands—made up a plate." He handed over the offering without making eye contact.

Why, he's actually blushing! thought Rebecca, amused and pleased. *He's not a bad fellow, really.*

"Thank you, Chester," she said, "and give my thanks to Blackie, too."

When nightfall turned very dark, she climbed into the loft and arranged her blankets on a thick bed of straw. The wind had come up outside and Rebecca felt chilly, but she heard distant laughter that drew her attention from the blankets. She searched the solid barn wall for a peephole and spied a small crack.

Rebecca lay on her stomach and peeked through. From an angle she could just see a corner of the big house. By the lantern light on the verandah, she observed several couples.

Is the taller man Coop? She couldn't see his face. The ladies were dressed in fancy gowns and bonnets. The colors of the dresses were indistinguishable in the faint light, but Rebecca could see they were stylish and elegant.

Maybe Chester is right. I won't fit in, she thought ruefully. She remembered the refined, fashionable Liza Wright, back home, and knew Liza would belong.

Well, better to heaven in rags than to hell in embroidery.

Rebecca turned away from her spying; she wanted to read her Bible for comfort, but she had no lantern. Then a verse sprang into her head and she said it aloud. "'For the love of money is a root of all kinds of evil. Some people, eager for money, have...pierced themselves with many griefs . . . .' Let that be a lesson to you, Rebecca Marie!" Exhaustion overcame her; she crawled into her bedroll and fell asleep almost immediately.

* * *

Rebecca awoke when the barn door squeaked on its hinges. A shaft of brilliant sunlight pierced the hayloft, illuminating the golden straw and the millions of tiny dust specks floating in the air. She heard footsteps on the packed dirt of the stable aisle, getting closer. There was a small pause, and then someone was climbing the loft ladder. Rebecca lay quite still, her heart pounding nervously.

"Mornin'," drawled Chester, before his head popped up over the edge of the loft.

Rebecca gave a sigh of relief. "Good morning to you, too."

"I 'spect ya might be wantin' breakfast. C'mon down to the mess house, I'll show ya the way. You'll be liken

Blackie's griddle cakes, they're the best 'round."

Rebecca glanced at her things.

Chester, apparently reading her mind, said "Yer gear's all right stowed up here fer awhile. T'aint no one gonna snoop round it."

He started back down the ladder and Rebecca followed. She stopped at the water trough and splashed icy water on her face.

"The hands already et," Chester said as they approached a long, low building. At the threshold he pointed to a big man in a food-spattered apron and said, "This here be Blackie."

Blackie nodded in silence. His hair and beard must once have been pure black but now were salted with white specks. Rebecca guessed him to be about sixty years old. His eyes seemed amiable in the fleshy face.

"This be the Reb," Chester said, pointing back at her with his thumb.

"Rebecca," she said.

"Heard about how you put Norm Kearn in his place," Blackie said in a good-natured tone. A big grin split his face.

Rebecca smiled. *They approve of me! They respect what I did with the whip.*

"Shore is good to have Coop back. He come out special this mornin' to make sure ya gets fed," Chester said.

Blackie added, "Said, after we fed you, you might help me and ol' Chester with our chores."

"Just till them fancy folks up ta the big house is gone," Chester inserted quickly.

The large room was filled with the delectable smells of melted butter and fresh-brewed coffee. Chester carefully lowered himself onto a bench at the long table. Blackie brought over a plate with pancakes stacked high and set it in front of Rebecca.

"I can only eat two," Rebecca said. She didn't want

to hurt Blackie's feelings.

"Naw, really, is that all?" he asked. "I wish them other fools would eat like that. Be a lot less work for me, eh?" and he winked.

Rebecca smiled again. She was going to like these two older men.

"Ya know," Chester said, "me and Blackie here practically raised Coop our own selves." He tipped his head toward Blackie, who sat opposite him. "Him and his pa couldn't see eye ta eye, so we taught the young pup most of what he knows."

Blackie nodded his big head in agreement, jowls shaking. He heaved his bulk up from the bench and lumbered to the cast-iron stove for a pan of brown-sugar syrup. He also grabbed a steaming pot of coffee and three tin cups before returning to the table.

Rebecca ate her pancakes slowly, listening as the two men gossiped. They spoke of Norm, the foreman, in derogatory terms. Then her interest was piqued when the subject changed to "the missus," Mrs. Conrad.

"She's a pushy mama, just a badgerin' them young uns. It ain't right," Chester said, shaking his head. "Poor Coop ain't got a chance. His mama will pester him into gettin' married, fer sure."

Blackie agreed mournfully. "The missus is gonna have that boy hog-tied before he can slip outta his boots." He blew into his cup and then took a noisy sip.

"She ought ta let nature take its own course," Chester said. They all bobbed their heads in agreement. "The missus is gonna chase the boy off again with her meddling ways, just like the ol' man done." He, too, slurped loudly of his hot coffee.

Chester continued. "Y'know, Coop always did have a' eye for the ladies, even as a young un. I 'member once he dropped a garden snake down the front of a little gal's dress just so's he could 'rescue' her in all her distress." Chester's pale blue eyes crinkled in his leathery face. He shook his head at the memory. "Took him a mighty long time to retrieve that serpent from her bosom, but somehow she found it in her heart to be grateful."

Rebecca tried to suppress a smile, but it tugged and curled the corners of her mouth.

"I'd best git," Chester said as he rose stiffly. "Ya gonna help Blackie in here awhile?"

Rebecca nodded and began to clear the table. The time passed quickly—Blackie entertained her with ranch stories, and she shared with him the workings of her farm. She really liked the hefty, affable man, she decided, and old, stooped Chester, too. They were ordinary, unremarkable men, but they were hardy souls strong enough to endure and carve out a living in this harsh land. She felt like one of them.

Later, when Chester came back for more coffee, Rebecca asked where the necessary was. Blackie stood at the door to point out the way to the nearest outhouse. Chester shouted to her retreating back, "I'll see ya at the barn. I fed the critters but we got ta muck out the stalls."

When she entered the stable, Chester handed her a manure fork and took one up himself. They busily pitched dirty straw from stalls into the center aisle as Madam chewed grain and watched them.

The pungent pile of manure and soggy, dark straw had grown large when Norm sauntered into the barn. He stopped dead at Madam's stall. Rebecca stared at him, waiting. His hair, the color of dirty bath water, was shaggy around the edges. His side whiskers were long and wispy, and his complexion was bad. She glanced at Chester, who cast darting looks at Norm between scoops.

"What do you think you're doing, giving expensive grain to your sorry critter?" Norm said. "It just gets hay and water. Even that's too good for it."

"I fed the cow," Chester said from the next stall. "The gal didn't."

"I'm the foreman here, old man, and until someone tells me different, you obey me." Norm stuck his thumb at Rebecca and continued, "She feeds her own and it gets just what I said, no grain." He turned on his heel and left the barn.

Chester grumbled under his breath and then he threw himself into his work.

They worked in silence until a heap of dirty straw stretched the length of the aisle.

"I best git a wheel barrow," Chester called from the opposite end of the stable. The squeaky door hinges signaled his departure.

Rebecca began to spread clean, shining straw in Madam's stall. The big barn door squealed again, and Rebecca looked up. In stepped another version of Liza, golden hair, elaborate dress and all. Cooper Conrad strolled beside her, and his arm was around her waist.

Chapter Six

"What kind of creature is this?" the blonde asked in a high, sing-song voice.

For a moment Rebecca thought she meant her, but they were staring at Madam.

"Oh, look at its sad eyes and droopy ears," the blonde continued with the same affected tone.

Rebecca nearly snorted at how phony the flirtatious girl sounded to her. But Cooper seemed to be drinking it in, standing there so tall and fine in his tailor-made trousers and matching vest. His full, black hair had been neatly combed, but a shining lock had fallen; it curved over his forehead pleasingly.

Rebecca was well aware that her own, braided hair hadn't been brushed since yesterday morning and her clothes badly needed washing.

Yago entered the barn with a small, dark-haired girl on his arm. The brunette was just as freshly dressed and primped as the blonde. Micah stepped in behind them.

"Millicent, come see this," called the first girl.

Cooper's girl, the pretentious, simpering one. thought Rebecca.

"What kind of cow is it?" asked Millicent. "I've

never seen one like this before. Daddy hasn't any like this."

Rebecca felt peevish and she couldn't stop herself. "It's a Brown Swiss milk cow and your daddy doesn't have one because he raises beef cattle," she said.

"You needn't be so rude, Reb," Cooper said. He turned to the coquettish blonde at his side. "Jezreel, we should probably return to the house. Your parents were about ready to leave when we began this little stroll."

Yago winked and smiled at Rebecca on their way out, and Micah came down the aisle to her.

"I finally found some interesting company, right here," he said, sighing and leaning on the gate of Madam's stall. "Those other girls are so witless and clingy," he said with a shudder. "How's Madam? Is she due for a milking?"

"Soon. I haven't had the time yet."

He opened the stall gate and came in. "Here, let me help you with that straw."

Rebecca's brow furrowed at what she was about to ask. "Have you or your brothers spoken with your mother about me yet?"

"Don't worry, everything will be fine," Micah said. He straightened, dusted off his hands, and said, "I'll go see to it now."

Chester returned with a wheel barrow just as Micah was leaving. The elderly man and the petite young woman returned to their odiferous work.

"You!" Norm suddenly hollered from the door. He jerked his head toward Rebecca. She tensed.

"You're s'posed to come up to the big house now." He waited as Rebecca walked stiffly toward him. He silently led the way through an opening in a thicket of lilac bushes. Then he dropped back, put his face close to her ear and spoke in a low voice. "You watch your back, missy. You never know what might happen . . . a little thing like you."

What did he mean by that? Was it a warning about Mrs. Conrad, or a threat?

A path led to the back door. When they entered, Rebecca saw it was a spacious kitchen with the largest iron cook stove she had ever seen. Standing at the stove was a stout, red-cheeked woman in a bleached feed-sack apron.

"Daisy, tell Mrs. Conrad she's here." Norm's harsh voice grated on Rebecca's taut nerves. The rotund cook left to do as Norm had ordered. Rebecca glanced at the tall, thin man and saw that he was looking her up and down. He chuckled perversely.

Rebecca waited uneasily, picturing the formidable Mrs. Conrad as a large, overbearing woman, perhaps brandishing a cane. She was surely a force of nature.

And how well I know the mayhem that Mother Nature can wreak, Rebecca thought. *One moment is filled with peace and productivity, and the next is . . . .*

Footsteps put an abrupt stop to her ricocheting reflections.

"So this is your homeless girl, Malachi." A dark-haired woman entered, with Micah and the short, round Daisy in close proximity behind her. Mrs. Conrad's piercing black eyes roved over Rebecca.

Why, she's only a few inches taller than me! Rebecca thought.

Mrs. Conrad's high cheekbones and full mouth made her an attractive woman. A softness that showed in her jawline, the slackening skin of her neck and the fine lines around her eyes were the only betrayals of her years. She was full-figured without being heavy. She wore a short black tea apron made of sheer fabric; an ivory fan hung at her waist that matched the creamy bodice of her dress and the off-white lace mantilla around her shoulders.

"Yago and Malachi speak highly of you, so there

must be more to you than I can see." Her penetrating gaze was an odd mixture of curiosity and doubt. "What are your abilities?"

"She can—"

"She can speak for herself, Malachi!" Mrs. Conrad said.

Rebecca detected a foreign sound to the woman's speech. With her exotic looks, her dress, she seemed novel, unique.

"I can do all household jobs and gardening," Rebecca said.

"We will give you a trial period of one week and then I shall make up my mind. If it works out, you can stay on for board and room." She sniffed the air with displeasure. "Daisy, get her a bath. She reeks of the barn."

Rebecca had listened, first with an impassive face, then a small, forced smile.

"Norm, I believe Cooper wishes to speak with you in the study." Mrs. Conrad turned to leave.

Micah stayed behind when his mother and the foreman left the kitchen. He ran to Rebecca and threw his arms around her in a hug.

"You can stay!" he shouted triumphantly. He released her when Daisy looked at them with one raised eyebrow.

The sturdy, kind-eyed woman took control. Rebecca was in Daisy's province now, and Daisy took her responsibilities seriously. She showed Rebecca where her quarters would be, right off the kitchen. The small room was filled with old chairs, several pails and shelves of cleaning supplies. On the wall hung a large zinc washtub.

Rebecca was somewhat befuddled. *I'm to board in the utility room?*

Daisy narrowed her eyes and surveyed the space.

"We'll remove some chairs and bring in a cot, and

you'll need a small chest of drawers. We'll hang a curtain there." She drew an imaginary line separating the household materials from the soon-to-be living area. "It'll be right cozy. Now, why don't you get two of those pails and fetch us some water for a nice hot bath for you. The cistern's out back."

Behind the house Rebecca discovered that fieldstones had been laid. Upon them rested a small, beautifully-wrought metal table. She was enthralled by its intertwining black leaves, flowers and vines. Two matching iron chairs completed the delightful setting. From that area, stepping stones led the way through arched alcoves and deeper into the wooded garden. The green scent of the plantings perfumed the air; the footpath was dappled with sunlight.

In one secluded spot, Rebecca was enchanted to find the marble statue of a beautiful woman. The chalk-white figure, several feet tall, gracefully stood atop a shell-shaped birdbath.

The charming scene captivated Rebecca, but she realized she mustn't stand gaping any longer. She forced her limbs to move, found the pump and cranked the handle as fast as she could, filling the two pails quickly.

Soon the water was warming in several massive kettles on the stove. Daisy put her hands on her ample hips.

"Now come and sit down while we wait for that to heat. We'll have us some tea and cake."

She bustled about and brought the fixings to the table. She pushed at her mouse-colored hair and asked, not unkindly, "Have you had a terribly hard time of things, dear?"

"There have been some difficult moments," Rebecca whispered. She looked at the dark amber tea in her cup, knowing that to meet Daisy's eyes would bring tears to her own.

Daisy changed the subject to cheerier topics and the two of them began to get better acquainted. The tea was strong and flavorful, the spice cake delectable. Rebecca was comfortable with this motherly middle-aged woman, and contented in her company. In a quiet moment when they both raised their cups for a sip, she heard footsteps approach.

A dark-eyed girl swept into the kitchen and smiled at them. Her arms were filled with a jumble of clothing.

"You're the new servant, yes? I'm Chalina."

Rebecca guessed her to be a few years younger than herself. *How pretty*, Rebecca thought, *with that glossy brunette hair fastened at the top of her head. She must be the sister, between Micah and Yago in age.*

"Call me Rebecca," she said.

"I'm keen on having another person in this house who is close to my age!" Chalina said rapidly, her words tumbling together. "Now, Mama and I dug through the very depths of my closet, and we came up with these for you."

Chalina dropped the pile on the table and picked out an olive green item, a dress. She held it up to her own slender body. The skirt was bell-shaped and full, the waist small, the collar high. Horn buttons ran down the back; there wasn't a single piece of lace to be seen.

"Cousin Katie handed it down. I never wear it. Much too drab for me. But see how it brings out your eyes!" Chalina held the dull green dress to Rebecca's cheek and Daisy agreed that, yes, indeed, it complemented her eyes. Rebecca caught the light scent of lavender emanating from the corded fabric.

Chalina prattled on.

"There's another of Katie's hand-me-down dresses here." It was a brown ocher color, no more decorative than the first, equally small in the bodice. "And I found a shimmy and several other things you might keep, if you like. Pantalettes, a corset, a petticoat, white stockings."

Rebecca disliked the feeling that monopolized her at the moment; she despised having to accept charity. *But I'll do what I have to do,* she berated herself.

Chalina's lovely heart-shaped face broke into a broad smile. "Welcome to the household," she said warmly. She flounced to the door and placed her hand on the knob. "Mama says you're expected in the drawing room when your bath is done. Daisy will show you the way."

* * *

The warm, soapy water had felt so good on her skin. She'd soaked and lathered and dunked as long as she'd dared. Now, her hair damp on her shoulders, Rebecca dressed in the clean underthings Chalina had given her. She slipped into the golden-brown dress; it was very snug around her hips and stomach and upper body, but it fit well enough.

She followed the round figure of Daisy through the house to the parlor, noticing along the way that the walls and ceilings of the home were finished smoothly. Some were clad in plaster alone and others were embellished with figured wallpaper.

Left alone to await Mrs. Conrad, Rebecca appraised the fine drawing room. It contained a divan and several chairs, all of fine, sturdy mahogany with burgundy-colored upholstery. The dark, polished wood was ornamented with deeply-carved foliage motifs. The thick wool rug underfoot featured pink and burgundy roses nestled amongst leaves of many shades of green. *How plush, how rich,* thought Rebecca.

A tall grandfather clock stood majestically against one wall, near a piano in the corner. The deep rose draperies were made of heavy brocade. Above the stone fireplace hung an oval-framed daguerreotype, the stiffly-posed portrait of an older man. Rebecca was drawn to it—the burly figure in the picture sat straight-backed and serious, staring into the camera unflinchingly. His hair was thick and wavy, as fair as Micah's. His rugged, handsome face wore a stoic expression. Rebecca was still studying the photograph when Mrs. Conrad entered.

The raven-haired woman wasted no time.

"Now, child, I will expect you to keep this house cleaned. Laundry should be your concern, too, rather than Daisy's. I expect all bedding to be laundered once a week. You can start with that today. Our guests have all gone, so you may begin with those rooms upstairs. On this floor, when you clean the study, do not touch any papers. Cooper specifically asked for the courtesy, and I wish to make that very clear."

"Yes, ma'am."

"You may go have an early lunch in the kitchen first, and then you may proceed." She patted her smooth black chignon and walked briskly from the room.

Daisy quickly produced a small meal, cold but delicious, and then she showed Rebecca the servants' stairs. They led from the kitchen to the upstairs hallway, which gave access to the bedrooms. Rebecca gathered up an armload of dirty linens and came back down the stairs. Daisy was not in the kitchen; in the quiet, Rebecca heard Cooper's deep voice from another room. He was joking and laughing with others of his family. She stood still for a few minutes listening to them, and then she picked up the pails and went to fetch more water.

* * *

Rebecca awoke to the brisk scratching of dry,

barren twigs against her dark window. The weeks had passed slowly since her trial period had been successfully surmounted. Summer had crossed into autumn with but one remarkable bit of news: an expedition led by Lieutenant Colonel George Custer had discovered gold in the Black Hills of Dakota Territory.

Daisy had repeated the gossip to Rebecca and added a prediction. "Mark my words, dear, there'll be a stampede, just like the frenzy in California 'n South Pass, too. Greedy people won't pay no mind to any treaty, 'sacred lands' or not." The older woman had shaken her mousy head and smiled dolefully.

Now, on her narrow cot, Rebecca listened to the *scritch-scritching* sound of branches on the window glass, her spirits low. She seldom saw the Conrad boys now, and she felt alienated from them, estranged. But Daisy was good to her, watched out for her, and Chalina was a friend.

How that girl babbles endlessly, though. I do miss the out-of-doors and the livestock terribly.

She arose, lit the lantern and crept to the parlor to peer at the clock. Four in the morning. She stood in the still, silent house, imagining she could hear her own heartbeat.

If I work very quietly, I could clean the study now, when no one's around, she thought. She noiselessly opened the study room door, spilling lantern light into the room. She nodded, making up her mind. She took her duties seriously. Her parents had labored hard from first light to last, every day, and they'd been happy. Sure, housework could be tedious, but Rebecca didn't mind hard work, especially if it took her mind off her own petty concerns.

Swiftly she padded back to her room and dressed before tiredness could seep back into her being. She brushed her hair, braided it, and then gathered cleaning paraphernalia. She returned to the study with her hands full and stood on the threshold for a moment before entering.

The room was Cooper's domain, and it intimidated Rebecca somewhat. It seemed to hold all the secrets of the Conrad family, financial and otherwise. She remembered well what Mrs. Conrad had said. "When you clean the study, do not touch any papers." Rebecca sighed.

This is ridiculous, to be in here cleaning when the rest of the world is asleep. But at least she wouldn't be in Cooper's way. During the day, he was in and out of this room at odd times.

She set to work on the bookcases that filled two walls. She pulled dusty leather-bound books off the lower shelves and wiped down both shelves and books before replacing them. Many of the books concerned botany, agriculture and animal husbandry. Rebecca thought she might ask permission to read some of them. Not the oldest, most scientific tomes, perhaps, but some of them. The days were growing shorter and colder; perhaps there would be time.

Mrs. Conrad had made it bitingly clear that Rebecca was not to associate with any of the Conrad men. Rebecca knew the cowhands would dig themselves in for the winter, nearly hibernating, and the three brothers would spend more time in the ranch house. How could she avoid them?

To be near Cooper more often. How difficult it would be. Those long legs, wide shoulders, that perfect jaw, and those eyes! Those reckless eyes, with tiny sparks in them. Yes, Coop's handsome face and exciting body were hard to resist. Many women, in fact, had been sorely challenged by his charm.

I'll allow I'm attracted to him. What if he realizes it? No. No, he'd never think of me in that way—he wouldn't even notice. There was no future for the two of them.

She placed her hand on her chest. *My heart is slowly being shattered by that man, bit by bit, and he doesn't even realize it.*

She began to sing her favorite hymn in soft, hushed tones as she worked.

> "Amazing Grace, how sweet the sound,
> That saved a wretch like me.
> I once was lost, but now am found,
> Was blind, but now I see."

In time she had to stand on tiptoe to reach higher shelves. She strode to the kitchen for the footstool, wobbly but usable, and fell into a rhythm with her task: Grab three books, clean the shelf, climb down, dust the books, climb up. And so it went—up and down on the precarious stool.

* * *

Upstairs, Cooper wakened from another fitful night. Disturbing thoughts of wills and weddings had tumbled through his head when he should have been sleeping soundly. Now he felt the urgent need to go to the privy, so he dressed quickly and stole down the dark stairs.

In a few minutes he came back into the house through the kitchen door, and stopped to raid the pantry for a piece of Daisy's cake.

Then he heard something—but what was it? He followed the gentle sounds to the study. A beautiful singing voice, in there! The door was ajar, and golden light filtered out. He stopped and strained to hear it again.

> "Through many dangers, toils and snares
> We have already come;

T'was Grace that brought us safe thus far
And Grace will lead us home."

Cooper peered through the doorway and saw Rebel, a bucket of water in one hand and a damp rag in the other, climbing a shaky stool. Cooper shoved through the door abruptly.

"Why are you cleaning in the middle of the night, Reb?" he whispered hoarsely.

Rebecca uttered a small cry and teetered on the stool. She reached out blindly, with the hand that still gripped a wet cloth, but found nothing but air. She lost her balance and toppled. The wash bucket drenched her. She lay in a pool of water, hair soaked, eyes and mouth wide open. Within a moment she jumped up nearly as fast as she'd fallen. She stood there sopping wet and glaring, with her fists on her small hips.

Cooper laughed softly at the spectacle. She looked so pitiful and adorable with her dripping pigtails and wet dress.

"Cooper Conrad!" rasped Rebecca. "You frightened me! You nearly made me break my neck. Now I have to clean up this mess and . . . and change my clothes."

"I didn't mean to startle you. I just wanted to know what you're doing in here at this hour of the night." He continued to chuckle.

"It happens to be morning."

It was true that a pale dawn had begun to leach into the darkness at the window. Distantly, the grandfather clock chimed the half-hour.

"That stool isn't safe," he said, changing the subject. "I'll make you a good, sturdy step-ladder."

Rebecca bent over to retrieve the pail and to right the stool. On hands and knees, she grabbed the rag and began sopping up water and wringing it into the pail.

Cooper stood over her and said, in a hushed tone, "You needn't work this hard. You're not going to be rewarded for extra labor."

He caught her under the arm and pulled her up to him, breathing in the scent of her—was it jasmine? He saw that her sodden dress revealed her figure admirably. The fabric was sticking stubbornly to her stomach, her legs, and to her bosom—the buds of her nipples stood up. Rebecca couldn't seem to meet his eyes. Head downcast, she looked as if she were being scolded. Cooper held her and began stroking the length of her arms, trying to give warmth and comfort. Her skin was as silken and luscious as pale butterscotch. He smoothed her still-dripping hair at the crown. The honeyed highlights from the summer sun were there yet.

He lifted Rebecca's chin with his forefinger until her face was tilted toward his. He gently touched the droplets that clung to her brow, her temple. He stroked her moist cheek and lightly—ever so lightly—skimmed her lips with his fingers.

Give me a sign, he pleaded inwardly, *a sign that you want to be close,* but Rebecca stood motionless under his caresses. She seemed oblivious. Cooper's own heart thudded and his breath caught, but she didn't respond to his touch. Her big, liquid eyes went to his and then darted away to the door. He released her and she bolted for the hallway.

Chapter Seven

Stupid, stupid! I behaved like a mute, frightened rabbit! Rebecca vilified herself. Her legs seemed unsteady as she ran to the sanctuary of her room. A shock had gone through her at Cooper's touch. Her heart had crawled into her throat. She was weak with wanting him.

She still trembled as she stripped off the saturated dress and soggy underthings and exchanged them for dry clothing. *I keep telling myself, over and over, to squelch these feelings, but my body doesn't comply!*

She stood a few more minutes, staring at the blowing branches scraping against the window glass. She'd frozen when he stroked her. *Perhaps that was a good thing. Cooper has had so many women, beautiful women. I won't be used like some trollop.*

She'd come very close to making a fool of herself. Resolved to display dignity and pride, Rebecca returned to the study determined to restore order to the scene of her fall. At the door, she heard Cooper's movements inside. He was still there. She entered the room with outward calm, but her heart was tripping over itself.

He sat at the big desk, ledgers and piles of papers

before him.

"Do you mind if I clean up this mess?" Rebecca's manner was diffident.

"Of course not, Reb. Please stay." He bent his head to his work again, in disregard, it seemed to her.

All right, I will, she thought. *I'll prove I'm not a scared rabbit.*

For a long moment they each worked in silence. Rebecca stubbornly dusted a few more shelves while Cooper shuffled through his papers. Finally he broke the stilted silence.

"For days now, I've been going through all this, comparing my father's records with more recent paperwork." He sighed and fingered a pile of documents. His forehead was creased with doubt.

Rebecca didn't know how to reply. She wished for the gift of facile speech, so she might respond with something smooth and light.

"You didn't get along with your father?" she asked, voice subdued.

Cooper shook his head.

"I left home at twenty. Partly because I had progressive ideas that my father didn't want to hear about. But a big part of it was . . . ." His voice faded away as he stared at nothing at all. Then he roused and went on. "My mother is an intense, fiery woman whom my father loved very much. She's of Spanish and Italian descent, hot-blooded and temperamental. I hated the way she manipulated Father. I thought a real man wouldn't allow himself to be dominated like that."

Rebecca was rendered speechless, stunned that Cooper would open up to her like that. *Say something, Rebecca, you dunce,* she rebuked herself. *Something wise and understanding.*

"I can hear Daisy stirring about. I must go help her."

* * *

Cooper watched her leave, stool and bucket in her arms. The bustle of her dress swayed gently and then she was gone. He rubbed his hands over his eyes, remembering their damp embrace, remembering their lips inches apart. He'd wanted her. She was to have been another conquest. A hundred women had thrown themselves at him, encouraging him, giving him their honor freely.

But she was different from those obliging women. She was no easy dancehall girl, no trollop he could bed without a second thought. Nor was she any longer the dusty farmer in men's clothes. She wasn't at all like some people in the settlement had made her out to be, not threatening or aberrant.

There was no denying to himself he'd had been aroused. By her taut little body. By her soft skin. By her eyes of that rare color. But there was more. He'd also felt tenderness. An affinity for the girl. For the *woman.* When she'd shown no interest, when she'd run off, it had hurt more than his pride.

It hurt his heart.

Yet, when she'd returned to the study, they'd been quite comfortable together. It was nice spending time with a woman who wasn't constantly chattering. Restful. Reb really was a hard worker. He couldn't visualize her sitting idle all day, gossiping with friends for lack of anything better to do.

The "acceptable" women his mother has been promoting as marriage material didn't possess the wifely qualities that—

No! I won't be hog-tied! He shook his head as if he felt the prodding of both his parents, jabbing him in the back. *Damn you, Dad, for putting that knife in my back, and Mother for turning it.*

Cooper stared at the cluttered desktop, ran a hand

through his thick hair and uttered another curse under his breath. A surge of emotion broke over him. He hadn't shared with anyone just how much he missed his father. Thoughts of the lost years brought a sheen of moisture to his eyes. He rubbed at them to clear his blurred vision. Then he took a deep breath and went back to studying ledgers and papers. There was something amiss with them; the numbers just didn't balance.

* * *

Rebecca stood shivering at her frost-patterned window. The snow-covered ground seemed as featureless as the leaden gray sky. A nursery rhyme popped into her head, and she spoke the words cheerlessly.

"The north wind doth blow
and we shall have snow.
What will the robin do then?
Poor thing.
He'll hide in the barn
to keep himself warm,
and hide his head under his wing.
Poor thing."

She studied the quiet, monochromatic landscape. Nothing moved.

"They hide in the barns and houses to keep themselves warm," she whispered. A gentle knock came at the door and Rebecca pushed through the separating curtains to answer it. Mrs. Conrad stood there, chin held high.

"The boys tell me that I must give you a day released from your duties. I don't see what you will do with the time, but you are free tomorrow. The holidays are upon us and soon we will be far too busy with the festivities to allow you to have time for yourself, so tomorrow it is."

"Thank you."

Rebecca watched Mrs. Conrad depart, her satin dress rustling, and then she heard raucous laughter from another part of the house. She listened to the deep murmur of male tones and pondered what she would like to do with her day of liberation. The men's noise seemed to recede as she considered. Spend more time with her beloved animals? She'd enjoyed taking Buster out for exercise ever since....

Her heart warmed to the memory of Cooper's kindness. He'd appeared at the barn one day while she was grooming the red horse. Her affection for the animal nearly rivaled her love for Madam. Coop had conversed with her in passing and added, almost as an afterthought, "Y'know, Buster's yours to use any time you want. In fact, he's yours, period."

How could one man be so complex? Heedless, yet also considerate; licentious one moment and so willing to share the next.

And now more kindness. A day of freedom. She felt an urge in her gut to see something different, to do something new. Tomorrow she'd like to go to Moskee's Trading Post. But how to get there? She didn't even know where it was.

She marched through the house seeking out Micah for his advice. She stood at the threshold of the kitchen; the room was hazy and redolent with cigar smoke. Her determination fled when she saw that all the Conrad men were seated at the table playing cards with Norman Kearn.

Micah saw her standing there reluctantly.

"Reb, have you come to shoo us out of here so you can clean?"

She felt her face grow warm.

"No, I came to ask your advice about my going to Mr. Moskee's place tomorrow. Can you give me directions?"

"So Ma has consented to give you a day off."

"Yes, but only after the boys told her to do it," she rejoined. She risked a glance at Coop, whose demeanor was quiet, reserved. Yago returned her gaze; his quick smile made his cheeks look pudgy.

Cooper turned his head toward the foreman. "Norm, you're going to Moskee Ridge tomorrow for supplies?"

"Yeah."

"You willing to give Reb a ride along?"

Rebecca shot a nervous glance from Cooper to Norm.

"Sure," he said, with a cloying grin.

Rebecca looked at the thin man with surprise. Why was he being so agreeable? He disliked her. Didn't he?

"What time will you be going?" she asked.

"Right after breakfast. It'll be cold, so you dress warm."

Back in her room, Rebecca lifted her mattress and retrieved some of the money Mr. Starns had paid her a lifetime ago.

* * *

At the kitchen table, Norm appeared to concentrate on his cards, but his mind was on Rebecca. He hadn't forgotten about their first encounter. On the contrary, he'd bided his time carefully, patiently, watching which way the wind would blow. He didn't want to lose his job over some little wildcat. His face burned, remembering the day she'd cracked that whip in front of his nose.

That gal's gonna pay for trying to make a fool out of me in front of the hands!

She'd been surprised at his friendliness tonight, he

could tell. *Good. She acts all innocent, all shy around men. Well, I'm gonna teach that little gal a lesson or two.* Something stirred in his blood, heating his loins. His mouth arranged itself into a wolf-like smile. *I'm going to like taming that little savage.*

Cooper interrupted his thoughts with a question, but Norm didn't hear. "What?"

"You got something weighing heavy on your mind?" asked Cooper with a chuckle. "I said, don't forget to pick up a new horse halter for me at the post tomorrow."

"Sure." Cards forgotten again, Norm's mind returned to the wench. *Yes, sireee!* He smiled to himself. *I'm really gonna enjoy teaching her what a real man is all about. And good ol' Coop, master of all, just opened the door for me.*

* * *

The next morning broke clear and raw. Rebecca was right on time, wrapped in an old, heavy cloak of Chalina's. Norm bundled her into the front seat of a large sleigh, tucking a buffalo robe around her legs.

The hour's ride to the trading post was enjoyable as the sled's runners flew across the stark white landscape. The snow-covered mountains wore beautiful shadows of blue-violet. The team pulling the sleigh began to steam as they trotted along, releasing their horsey smell. Even the sharp, pure air striking Rebecca's hot face felt good. She was nonplussed to find Norm a pleasant-enough companion.

At the general store, Norm handed the proprietor his list of needed supplies while Rebecca wandered about, looking at everything. Barrels, bags and crocks filled with goods. Knives, axes, shovels and more. She rounded the corner of one aisle and saw a cage of live chickens. The sign read, "Five laying hens and one rooster for one dollar."

Rebecca wanted those chickens and she had a silver dollar to pay for them. She found Norm and excitedly pulled on his sleeve, tugging him toward the cage. "I would like to buy them, and have fresh eggs in the spring."

Norm's lips curled into an odd smile. "Sure thing. I betcha Chester'll make a cage for them at one end of the granary."

Rebecca smiled and walked off to make those chickens hers.

* * *

Rebecca and Norm returned to the ranch with supplies, a cage full of chickens, and what appeared to be cordiality between them. Maybe they were *friends* now, Cooper thought glumly.

Chester set about building a chicken coop immediately, although it was Cooper's feathers that were ruffled. He stewed and complained the entire time he watched the old man work.

"First the cow, then poultry! Can you believe Norm let her bring chickens here? This isn't a damn farm!" Cooper grumbled.

"You gotta admit Blackie's cookin' has improved since Reb brought that cow," Chester said. "And ain't it a good thing, ol' Norm bein' nice to the gal?"

"More than likely he's just thinking of getting under her skirts." Cooper's tone was ugly. The discord he felt was new and strange for him.

Chester threw a surprised look at Cooper. "You sure that ain't yer own thoughts, boy?"

"No, old man. My tastes don't run to scrawny little girls. But I heard some things about Norm that make me wonder where his tastes run."

"You better watch him with that girl, then." Chester scowled, concern for Rebel written all over his face. It was clear he didn't like the idea of Rebecca being hurt or, worse, ruined.

"I'm not her nursemaid." Cooper turned on his heel, leaving Chester to finish the coop in silence.

* * *

Two weeks later, when Norm had to make another supply run for Mrs. Conrad, he asked Rebecca to go with him again. She said yes and went without permission. She confided to him that she didn't think Mrs. Conrad liked her very much, nor would she have allowed her this outing.

Norm's smile was ingratiating. He knew the game was going his way—he'd visited with the little tease every day, real sociable-like, and she trusted him.

They arrived at the post around noon. Norm casually mentioned, "Y'know, Mrs. Moskee offers meals to them that can pay. It'll be my pleasure." His voice made his voice sound smooth and easy. Rebecca was susceptible—her face lit up at the idea.

Seated at a small table, Rebecca said, "I've never done anything like this before."

Norm chuckled at her backwardness. "The Conrad folks are served their supper all the time. But even us lowly folks can get treated like the lofty man, if we got money to buy it."

He studied Reb's animated face as she looked around her. She was too intent in ogling her surroundings to take note of his smirk of satisfaction. *You will pay for this meal and everything else you owe me, little girl,* he promised himself. He felt his maleness harden with anticipation. Tonight

When they arrived back at the Conrad ranch, Rebecca was loath to go to the ranch house, reluctant because she hadn't been given permission to leave in the first place. She loitered in the barn and helped Norm put things away. They bedded down the team and curried them. Norm finished brushing his horse first and came to stand beside Reb.

Slowly, deliberately, he took the horse brush out of her hand and put it down.

"I think that's good enough."

With a calculated move, he tucked an errant strand of her hair behind her ear and then suggestively ran his fingers down her neck. He put one arm around her and bent down to put his mouth on hers. He held her tight with one hand and reached under her cloak with the other, groping, grasping, clamping onto her breast.

She struggled against him and his body tensed in response. He was breathing heavily, clutching at her clothing.

Rebecca whimpered.

"No!" she cried as she pulled her mouth away from his. She gasped for breath.

* * *

"What's goin' on here?" Chester demanded. He had approached unnoticed. It looked to him like Norm had the little gal in a clinch.

"Nothing that concerns you, old man" Norm said.

"Figured I'd better come check on that cow to see if she's been milked. Good thing I did. You better leave that girl alone, boy."

Rebecca stood immobilized, a look of mortification on her deeply reddened face.

"Go on up to the house, little girl. I'll take care of the cow for you."

Chester watched as the girl obeyed.

Reb ran for the barn door, glancing back apprehensively when she reached it. Then she dashed across the shadowy yard and under the bare lilac branches. A stream of light from the open kitchen door came and went.

Norm kept his mouth shut. Chester hadn't seen much, but now he stood with his arms crossed, stubbornly watching Norm, whose mouth was white with anger. He stalked out, turning in the narrow confines so he wouldn't have to touch Chester. From the looks of it, Norm was up to something. Chester worried that Norm would be out for revenge.

* * *

Rebecca entered the quiet, deserted kitchen and hurried directly to her curtained sanctuary. She struggled out of several layers of clothing and threw herself on her paltry bed. Her body was radiating the heat of embarrassment, and she was tormented by guilt. For Chester to see her in such a compromising situation—Chester, whose respect she valued so much! And she was guilty of being rebellious to Mrs. Conrad, after she'd kindly taken her in. Why, Rebecca thought with chagrin, she was even guilty of forgetting to milk her precious Madam!

But there was something about Mrs. Conrad, Rebecca reminded herself, something that made her want to defy the woman just as she'd done people back in Dakota Territory.

She knew she would have to apologize to Mrs. Conrad first thing in the morning.

She couldn't keep her mind from turning in bewilderment to the skirmish with Norm. Her first kiss. Not tender and loving, but rough, sloppy, hurtful. With his face in hers, the pockmarks on his cheek had seemed as big as craters. When Chester walked in on them, Norm's face had been a mask of white-hot anger.

Rebecca fell asleep with tears clumping her lashes and dampening her pillow.

* * *

"Daisy, is Mrs. Conrad really upset with me? I'll go and apologize right away."

"Lord, child, you've got this house shining like it's never been before. She and her daughter were off visiting yesterday, dragging those poor boys with them. No one knew you were gone, so don't say a word about it."

"Oh, thank God!" Rebecca sighed, relaxing visibly. She vowed to herself she would never commit such an act again; it was too draining.

There was a knock at the kitchen door and Daisy answered it. Blackie stood there holding a plucked and gutted chicken in one oversized hand.

"What in the world? That wouldn't be one of Reb's chickens, now, would it?"

"I didn't do it," Blackie put in quickly, his extra chins quivering. "It weren't nobody's fault—it was an accident."

Rebecca, face lowering, came to the door reluctantly.

"The rooster," Blackie said, as Rebecca peered at the white, pimpled remains.

"My rooster! I only had one. He was downright pretty, too. What happened to him?"

"It will be a story long in the tellin'."

"Then you better sit down and tell it," Daisy said, taking charge. She took the bird and put it in a large bowl of freshly drawn well water. Rebecca poured coffee for them and Blackie heaved his bulk onto a chair at the kitchen table.

"It was Norm." He pointed a thick finger at Rebecca. "Now, don't get all steamed up, girl. It was an accident, like I says before."

"How can you be so sure?" Rebecca challenged him, raising her chin. "He may be getting back at me for what happened last night."

"I seen it. It all has ta do with a man's winter underwear. If it was anyone's fault, it would be Micah's dog's fault. Duke done it." Blackie nodded his head for emphasis.

"I don't see how the shooting of one of Reb's chickens has anything to do with men's winter underwear and a dog," Daisy said. "And what happened last night?"

"Never you mind," replied Blackie quickly. "Norm just got a little cheeky and Reb here didn't like it none."

Daisy's ruddy face clouded. "He means trouble for her. I don't like him."

"This is not telling me about my rooster."

Blackie delivered a considerable sigh.

"If you'd keep your traps shut I might be able to." He looked at them both and, after a moment of quiet, continued. "I think he was tryin' ta get on the good side of you. All he was gonna do was check on them there chickens cuz he heard a lot of squawking."

"When did this happen?" asked Rebecca.

Blackie shot her another stern look.

"Last night, Norm found himself a jug and got tittered. He was feeling pretty jolly by the time he went ta bed. He woke up in the middle of the night, prob'ly to go relieve hisself, and he heard a ruckus with them chickens. I'm a light sleeper and I heard it, too. So I watched what he was up to. He took the rifle and went out in his union suit and boots."

Blackie rubbed his jowls with a beefy hand, and continued. "When Norm opened the granary door, he had the rifle pointin' in, gettin ready ta aim. Well, the poor sucker was missin' a button on his flap—you know, the one in the back. So the flap folded open a mite, exposing the man's arse. Micah's dog came sneakin' up behind Norm and stuck his cold nose inta Norm's open flap. That cold nose touchin' him, it ain't no wonder he pulled the trigger!"

Daisy put her hand to her ample bosom as she gasped with laughter.

"I thought it downright funny my own self," Blackie said, "until I saw him carryin' that rooster back. I dressed it right away for you. Norm seems to be powerful sorry about it."

Rebecca looked at the two of them and sighed. "I suppose one should look for the humor in it." She smiled a little and then remembered there would be no chicks come spring. She'd been hoping that when the hens laid more, she could hatch out one batch of chicks to increase her flock and then sell the rest of the eggs at Moskee's. Now, thanks to Norm, that wouldn't happen.

Don't ever sell the bearskin before you've caught the bear, she thought sadly. "I wish he would have killed a hen instead."

Chapter Eight

"Cooper!" Martina called imperiously from the dining room.

"In here, Mother," Cooper muttered through a mouthful of gingerbread. He strode to the doorway to intercept his mother.

"I want to speak with you, about the Christmas party your sister and I are planning."

Cooper groaned. "Another tea party?"

"A large Christmas party, with music and dancing. I want plenty of young people here. Perhaps if you see all the available young ladies together, you will be able to make a choice. After all, Jezreel doesn't seem to be appealing to you, even though you do have the reputation of being another Don Juan Ternorio."

"Mother, stop pushing. I'll find my own wife in my own time."

"I don't want you to lose this ranch, Cooper. Your father and I had hopes that our firstborn would also be the first to carry on the family name. I feel that you aren't taking things seriously. But lawyer Dunn assures me that it is very serious. He seems to be watching all this with great interest. I cannot understand why, but he is. He also seems to be pushing for Jezreel's hand himself, and he appears to be winning. If only you would show the girl more interest, I'm sure she would stay with you."

"Jezreel is snobbish, arrogant and conniving. David Dunn can have her."

"Cooper!"

"No more, Mother!" Cooper said. "Have your party, but don't push. I'm warning you. Believe me, I love this land and I'll handle it in my way."

* * *

Norman Kearn seethed with anger. He stood at the bunkhouse window, apart from the others, watching the snowfall through icy panes. Gusts of wind threw flurries and built drifts in its path. Nothing else moved out there, quiet under a thick blanket of snow. He listened to the other men, laughing and joking amongst themselves. Their fellowship with each other—but not with him—it rankled.

Never had a pot to piss in, he thought miserably, until old man Conrad died. I had to take what I wanted . . . wasn't gettin' it any other way. Sure, I've gambled some, but I give cash to Dirty Marie, too. And not just to bed her, neither, although now she won't lift her skirts without it. She needed the money, her and her boy. And Norm knew what life was like for the bastard son of a penniless woman. It had been more than a month since Norm had made the trek to Gaspar and to Dirty Marie's. He needed a woman bad.

A movement out there in the whiteness caught Norm's eye. It was Reb, emerging from the granary. She carried a milk pail and a basket. Norm knew the girl would follow her routine—she'd gathered eggs first; now she'd go to the barn to milk the cow. Lascivious excitement was growing inside him. The slut owed him and today would be pay day. His rock-hard member would not be denied.

* * *

Rebecca sat on a little stool close to Madam enjoying her warmth. She had washed the udder and placed the pail directly in front of the cow's back feet. She leaned her head against the light brown flank, feeling the softness of Madam's hide against her cheek. She smelled the sweet odor of the animal and felt at home. Her mind lulled as she began the milking rhythm.

Outside, the winter wind howled, but here was calm and repose. Her hands, placed tightly up against the bag, each gently squeezed a teat. She pulled the milk down, the streams making hollow metallic sounds as they hit the bottom of the empty pail. The tin vessel quickly filled with hot milk and the rhythmic, drum-like sounds became softer.

Nothing was audible but the plopping sound of milk joining with that already in the pail. The spurts of milk got smaller until they ended altogether. Rebecca stood, looked at the amount in the pail, and told the cow, "You're drying up." She hung the half-filled pail on a nail and put the stool in the corner.

"She'll have to be bred and have a calf to give more milk."

Rebecca whirled at the sound of Norm's voice.

"Yes, she will." At the gate she shot him a sharp, testy look. "I have to get hay."

Norm nodded his head once and opened the stall to let her pass through. He followed her to the ladder of the hay loft.

Rebecca felt a prickle of apprehension crawl up her spine, but brushed it off. It was odd, she thought, his following her like that. *What does he want?*

"I'll help you. A person gets mighty bored without

anything to do," Norm said.

Rebecca shrugged, hearing a false friendliness in his voice. He followed her up the ladder.

In the loft, she saw the pitchfork a few feet away, its tines buried deep in hay. Before she could reach it, the world erupted into sickening confusion.

She was thrown to the floor. Pressing weight fell on top of her. Fear knifed into her. Couldn't breathe. She struggled. Kicked. Fought.

Norm breathed wetly, hotly, into her face, panting. He held her down. Her resistance only excited him. Rebecca pushed and thrashed furiously. He ground his body into hers even harder, mashed his mouth on hers and sucked hard on her lower lip. It felt like he was sucking her blood out through her pores.

"Aaoww!" she cried. His hand clamped down over her mouth. It smelled strongly of tobacco and lamp oil. She worked an arm free, reached up and pulled at his unkempt hair.

"You ain't much without that whip of yours, are you, missy?" Norm said. He grabbed the hair at the back of *her* head and jerked hard.

Rebecca tried to scratch his face; he seized her wildly flailing hand in one of his own and yanked her head back again with the other. His bloodshot eyes glinted with cunning.

Viciously he ripped her cloak open, tearing the buttons off.

"No!"

"Shut up! You're gonna like this."

With stained fingers, he savagely tore at the top of her dress, scratching her neck.

"Stop it!"

She fought to free her hands and legs, wriggling, squirming like a wild thing.

Norm pinned her hands together over her head and pulled her skirts up with his free hand. She felt the shock of cold air on her exposed legs. He reached down and began pinching and touching her where his foul, filthy hands should never be. He pulled down her pantalettes; his hand on her stomach was moist, clammy.

"No!" It was a mournful, hopeless wail that echoed throughout the deathly-quiet stable. She began bucking to rid herself of him, but he was too heavy. Rebecca gasped in her effort to breathe.

Norm was fumbling with his belt buckle when he was hoisted off her with a great heave.

"You bastard," Cooper said with a snarl. He drew his arm back and, with the crack of knuckles hitting jaw and the brutal grinding of bone on bone, sent Norm's gaunt figure sprawling. Cooper stood over him, eyes snapping with malevolence.

"Git! Gather your gear and get off this place now."

Cooper stepped back just enough to allow the pole-axed Norm to regain his footing. He never took his eyes off the weaving cowboy as Norm staggered to the loft opening and scrambled down the ladder.

When Cooper turned to Rebecca, she'd come to a sitting position and gathered her skirt about her trembling legs. She wiped moisture from her cheeks with shaking hands, but her eyes remained bright with tears.

"Come, now," he said gently as he knelt beside her. "He isn't gonna hurt you ever again." He petted her head, soothing her as if she were a frightened puppy.

"I—I—di—didn't d—do anything to provoke him." Her voice was strangled and thin. Spasms shook her body. She felt deep shame to her very marrow.

Cooper gathered her into his muscular arms and pressed her head to his warm, protecting chest.

"I know," he soothed. "From the talk in Gaspar, you weren't the first he's mistreated." He began to pat her back as if she were a child. "I was going to fire him anyway. That's why I came looking for him just now. I discovered he was swindling money from us. Selling Conrad stock and supplies on the sly, tampering with bills of sale, doctoring receipts."

Rebecca lifted her head from the cradle of his arms and looked at him with her eyes still swimming. Her nose ran and she sniffled.

Cooper's comforting tone turned grim, "I would have delivered him to the law, but if I had to look at his ugly face one minute more, I'd have killed him with my bare hands."

His eyes had flashed briefly but then he looked down at her and they turned to soft dark chocolate again. He gave her a hug and assisted her to her feet and down the ladder. He helped her gather the milk pail and egg basket and escorted her back to the house. The air outside was so cuttingly cold it hurt to breathe. The wind picked up lashings of snow and threw it at them as they made their way.

* * *

The new day sparkled, fresh and beautiful.

"My little *rosa*, isn't the weather perfect for a party?" Martina joined her daughter by the window and hugged her.

Cooper watched sourly from his chair. *She never quits,* he thought dully. His mother was a willful woman who, in the midst of parties and social gatherings, played the part of the grand Mrs. Conrad expertly and demanded no less from her children.

He wished it were spring so he could be out looking after strays and calving cows. He planned to slip out later to see that the ice at the watering hole had been chopped open.

The faint tinkling of sleigh bells floating through clear, crisp air.

"Someone's here already!" Chalina said as she wrapped her shawl snugly around her and ran to the door. Several cowhands were there to help with satchels, sleigh, and horses. Cooper took up a post in the hallway. Begrudgingly.

"Carmella, come in!" Chalina's thick, lustrous hair was arranged around her shoulders; she tossed it as she beckoned to her mousy friend. The two girls minced into the warm house arm in arm and began yammering about the latest gossip.

More sleigh bells chimed in the still morning air. More visitors. The guests would stay for the night, some sleeping on pallets on the floor. Soon the house was filled, and, except for Cooper, cheerful. In nearly every room, people chatted, laughed, ate, drank and celebrated. The house was decorated with evergreen boughs, cranberry and popcorn garlands, and ribbons. The Christmas tree in the parlor wore bits of colored paper, yarn ornaments and glass baubles. Fireplaces blazed and crackled and candles flickered everywhere. The air smelled of wax, furniture polish and pine.

Cooper heard the tinkle of piano keys, but he felt removed from the festivities. His mind was far from the party. He couldn't forget the afternoon in the loft. Reb's pallid face, her huge, glassy eyes. He'd felt such an overwhelming tenderness toward her, a sentiment he'd never have admitted to in the past.

And yet, even as he consoled her and was so moved by her, he'd wondered. Had she led Norm Kearn on? Women could be so deceptive. Oh, he could understand why a man would desire her, with those jewel eyes, and skin the peachy golden color of ripening apricots.

Where was she, anyway? Why wasn't she helping with the party?

Chapter Nine

Rebecca slipped out to the barn for a moment of tranquility. She'd helped Daisy cook for the feast to come and all the treats in between. They'd made gingersnaps, peanut brittle, popcorn balls and more. She'd also prepared all the bedrooms, even though they were already without a speck of dust. Now she needed a moment to herself.

She thought wistfully of putting on her old clothes and going riding. Then she touched the scratch at the base of her throat and allowed anger to interrupt her quietude. She hated Norm for what he'd tried to do. But she was furious with herself, too. She'd been foolish. Trusting. Before, she'd always been able to handle come what may. She'd never be naive about men again.

She stroked Madam's soft, pale muzzle and then traced the line of light-colored hairs that ran down the cow's back. Suddenly the serenity, the solitary hush, was broken.

"Rebel, Mother wants you," called Yago. "I believe she wants you to serve some of Daisy's hot mulled apple cider."

Rebecca looked down at the skirts of her worn

green dress. "Do I look all right in this?"

"You look fine, Rebel. If anyone gives you a hard time, just send them to me." Yago puffed his strapping chest in mock bravado.

Rebecca entered the house through the back, washed up and began filling mugs with cider. She balanced a tray of the spicy, steaming drinks in both arms and began to thread her way through the crowded hall. Through the open door to the drawing room she overheard the small brunette, Millicent, talking with lowered voice as if she were divulging a secret.

"I think it's awful, the way Jezreel is playing Coop and David against each other."

Rebecca recalled the pretentious blonde, Jezreel, from that day in the barn months before. She couldn't help herself—she had to stop and listen.

The girl just inside the door, the one with whom Millicent was sharing rumors, was Chalina's plain friend Carmella.

"I think if Mrs. Conrad would stop pushing at Cooper, he would have asked Jezreel to marry a long time ago. But you know how bull-headed he can be," Carmella said.

"You may be right, and I have an idea that David knows, too," Millicent said. "In fact, I think David will present her with a ring this Christmas."

"Do you think she'll accept it?"

"I believe she will. She'll do it just out of spite, even though she obviously thinks Coop's the better catch."

"Why would she do it out of spite?" asked Carmella doubtfully.

"Because, my dear, she's been fishing for Cooper ever since he's come back, and she's made no headway. Her pride has been injured."

An older couple stopped to take two mugs of cider from Rebecca's tray. Soon she'd have to return to the kitchen for more. For now, though, she couldn't resist eavesdropping.

"Micah told me there was a girl in Dakota Territory he really liked," whispered Carmella conspiratorially.

"You don't think it's that serving girl? Mrs. Conrad seems to be nervous about her and Cooper."

"Are you joking? What would he see in that wallflower? Really, Mill, you do have an imagination."

"Mrs. Conrad—Martina—has told me herself she is worried about the relationship between Coop and that girl," replied Millicent with heat. "I know what I'm talking about."

Rebecca didn't wait to hear any more.

Mrs. Conrad thinks Cooper has feelings for me? Rebecca nearly laughed at the absurdity of the idea.

Rebecca still had two full cups on her tray. She glued a smile on her face and entered the parlor.

"Would you ladies care for some cider?"

The two beautifully gowned girls accepted the cups, eyeing Rebecca's dowdy dress. Carmella didn't even try to disguise her disdain, and her scornful glance did not escape Rebecca's notice. *A tree is known by its fruit, not by its leaves,* she told herself righteously.

With a toss of her head, Rebecca stomped back toward the kitchen for more cider. On the way, she nearly bumped into Cooper. He looked splendid in a tailored coat with woolen trousers of the same dark fabric, superb with his black hair. She was near enough to smell his pleasant soapy scent. She looked down, unable to meet his eyes. He held out his arms but she ducked around him, and heard a male guest tease Cooper derisively.

"They say you have what all the women want, Conrad, but you can't even capture the maid."

"What's your problem, David? What have I ever done to you?" Rebecca heard aggravation in Cooper's voice.

Her quick glance back revealed a stiff-backed athletic figure with wavy blond hair and a cold face.

So that's David, she thought.

The revelers became more noisy, the celebration more rollicking as the day progressed into evening. A fiddler and a man with a mouth organ accompanied the pianist in providing dance music. Rebecca noticed that Jezreel hung on David's arm as if glued to his side. But she also saw the blonde throwing furtive glances at Cooper, glances filled with resentful hurt.

Rebecca was aware, too, of Martina's angry glaring at her son. Coop did seem remote and distant tonight. She guessed the woman wanted Coop to stop being so aloof, to mingle with the guests. Later she saw that he'd turned to the uncomely Carmella for company, seeming to hang on her every word.

Probably to appease his mother, Rebecca told herself.

* * *

Late that evening there was more speculation behind the door of the bedroom that Chalina and Millicent were sharing for the night.

"Did you notice how Cooper paid attention to Carmella?" asked Millicent.

"Yes, and I wonder what he sees in her. I've found her to be uncharitable and less than kind sometimes."

"Well, she does have a good figure."

"Did you see Mama's eyes light up when she saw they were cozy?"

"I think everyone saw that."

"I don't think Carmella's father was too happy about it, though."

"Why do you say that?" asked Millicent.

"Apparently he's heard of Cooper's reputation as a rascal with the ladies. I heard him talking about it with

Yago." Chalina's voice became teasing. "Speaking of Yago, I saw him snuggling up to a certain little brown-haired friend of mine."

"You know how I feel about him, don't you?" Millicent asked dreamily. She yawned, somnolent. "As for a lady for Cooper, I guess I like Carmella better than Jezreel."

"The lesser of two evils," replied Chalina sleepily.

* * *

It was Christmas Day. Rebecca stood idly by the kitchen window watching small snowflakes whisk by. "I wonder what became of Norm?" she asked.

"Best get that no-good outta your mind, missy," Daisy scolded. "He won't be back."

Daisy had tried to warn her about him, Rebecca remembered. She claimed to be a good judge of character, and said she'd had to be, after leaving her no-good bum of a husband years before.

Daisy had just one tiny shortcoming. She hoarded food. The most succulent parts of a roast, the last wedge of pie, she secreted for herself and now that Rebecca was under her wing, for her, too. Rebecca found it easy to pardon the pudgy woman's small weakness, especially when she herself benefited.

"What are you giving the Conrads for Christmas, Daisy?"

"I knitted everyone a scarf this year," she said, nestling utensils into a stack of bowls. "Last year I knitted the boys socks, and mittens for Chalina and the missus. What about you, Reb, what are you giving them?"

"I made chokecherry jam this fall and decorated the jars up real pretty. Do you think they'll mind getting jam?"

"Not at all. How many jars have you?"

"I made up twelve jars."

"That will be a nice gift. Nothing too personal." Daisy noticed Rebecca's inquiring look and added, "At least no one can read anything into it."

"What do you mean?"

"The missus thinks there's something between you and Cooper. She thinks that's why he doesn't turn to 'the right kind of girl'." Daisy rolled her eyes.

"That's absurd! He doesn't see anything in me but a nuisance."

"Apparently he's been giving you some attention. She says she's seen it herself, him watching you."

"I still say that's ridiculous. She's barking at shadows. She doesn't like me much and is using that as an excuse."

"Never mind, child. Help me ready these refreshments. You look right nice—take care you don't spill on that pretty dress."

The day before, Christmas Eve, Chalina had asked Rebecca to her room for a "girl's dress-up," as she'd called it. They'd taken turns pinning each other's hair up in a number of styles, experimenting with twists, ringlets over the ears and more. When the chatty girl had stood behind Rebecca, brushing her hair for her, she'd remarked that it had darkened over the months. It was still shot with thin strands of gold and red on the top layers, but a sleek seal-brown underneath.

Rebecca had stared into the looking glass, remembering her father's blue-black locks. *Why couldn't I have inherited his hair color instead of this aquiline nose?* she'd asked herself. She'd been a little ashamed to think it.

"Pour the nog into that pitcher, would you?" Daisy asked. She waddled about the kitchen happily, in her element.

Rebecca poured with painstaking accuracy, mindful of the fine frock she wore. Yesterday Chalina had presented her with it: a lovely dress of dark yellow-green silk, with rows of ribbon on the skirt. Rebecca had touched the opulent, moss-colored material longingly.

"It's wonderful, but I can't accept it. What would your mother say?"

Chalina's big, reassuring smile made her dimples even deeper.

"All my friends have seen me wear it far too many times. And Mother has promised me a deep blue taffeta; my armoire is stuffed as it is! Now, about some shoes."

Daisy interrupted Rebecca's reverie.

"It's time we joined the family for our part in Christmas."

Daisy carried the Christmas pudding. Rebecca, her silk dress rustling, followed with the eggnog and cups. The Conrads were already gathered in the parlor. The family's own, private gift exchange was done and the items were scattered about the room.

Rebecca became aware of an odd roil of feelings. Her cheeks flushed hotly. She didn't belong here. She missed the Christmases she'd shared with her parents. The sharply-pointed toes of Chalina's shoes pinched her feet.

Cooper, wearing a beautiful brown velveteen jacket, sat near the tree.

"Here, Rebel, let me help you with that," he said as he jumped up to take the pitcher of eggnog from Rebecca. He allowed his hand to linger on hers for a heartbeat.

His gentlemanly action was like a direct hit to the ribcage after what Daisy had said in the kitchen. Rebecca's eyes flew immediately to Mrs. Conrad and she saw a scowl appear. She quickly moved away from Cooper and sat in a corner, apart from any of the brothers.

It was a reaction that caused Cooper to send guarded looks her way. It seemed he didn't miss a thing: his mother's glowering face, Rebecca's avoidance of him and her discerning glances at his mother.

"Well, Daisy, what have you got for us this time?" asked Yago, oblivious to the emotional undercurrents flowing around him.

Daisy waggled a plump arm amongst the packages under the tall tree and withdrew her gifts. She distributed them to everyone. There was even a scarf for Rebecca. When enough attention and appreciation had been given to her gifts, Daisy said, "Now it's your turn, Reb."

Rebecca brought out a large covered sbasket and set it in the middle of the room.

"This is for all of you."

"Micah, why don't you do the honors," Mrs. Conrad said.

Micah unwrapped the cloth from the top of the basket to reveal the jars nestled there like sparkling red jewels.

Rebecca's face burned as she heard the murmurings of "Thank you," "How nice," and "Marvelous."

"Did you make these yourself, Rebel?" asked Cooper. At the nod of her head he continued. "Then I'll have to sample some as soon as possible."

Rebecca noted the return of Martina's dour expression. *It doesn't mean what you think*, she wanted to shout to the apprehensive woman.

She handed a small bundle to Daisy.

"This is for you," she said, ducking her head.

The hearty woman beamed with pleasure when she unwrapped the organdy tea apron.

"Mr. Moskee had a remnant of the material at the trading post," Rebecca said.

Mrs. Conrad chose that time to take up the heavy

skirts of her ornately trimmed purple dress and hand out Christmas bonuses—silver dollars—to her servants. Daisy was rewarded with four of them to Rebecca's one. It was only right, Rebecca knew, since Daisy had been with the family for a long time.

Then Martina instructed loftily, "Chalina, pour out the eggnog for everyone. Micah can hand out the pudding."

Cooper quietly left the room and returned shortly, carrying a new six-foot stepladder. A big red ribbon was tied to the end of one finely crafted leg. He propped it beside Rebecca and looked deep into her eyes.

"This is the ladder I promised you, Rebel."

"Thank you, Mr. Cooper." she said. It was just a workman's aid, she reprimanded herself, an implement for a laborer, nothing more. But she couldn't keep hope down. *Shared secrets . . . the wobbly stool, the embrace. . . . He was thinking of me and the time we were alone together in the study.*

Rebecca threw another glance at Martina and saw questioning and pique written on her face. She swallowed hard.

"What a thoughtful idea," Chalina complimented her older brother.

"Well, I have some news," put in Yago. His stout chest seemed to puff up even more. "I have asked Millicent to be my wife, and she said yes!"

Squeals and congratulatory back-slapping ensued. Martina gave her second oldest son a hug and a kiss.

"This calls for a celebration," Cooper said, grinning wildly. He rose to fetch the wine bottle, and Daisy accompanied him to get the glasses.

"You know what this means, don't you, Daisy?" Barely audible, he whispered, "Now Mother is going to redouble her efforts on my behalf."

Chapter Ten

It was so good to be out on the sorrel's back, inhaling the perfume of fresh March air and feeling the weak spring sun on her face,. A light breeze was blowing, and scattered patches of snow were quickly melting. Life was good; Rebecca felt invigorated. She had put on her father's clothes for the ride, and she wore her whip for protection.

In her exhilaration, she rode far from the ranch house. There was so much to see and to enjoy. She nosed the horse up a rolling, forested hillside. They came upon a stream running fast and clear. That's when Buster bolted, throwing Rebecca to the ground hard and knocking the wind out of her. The startled horse left her lying on the firm, moist earth.

When she could breathe again, Rebecca moved her limbs and heard a deep growl, like nothing she'd heard before. Fear flooded her chest. Her heart pounded. She froze. She heard a lower, quieter rumble and the shuffling of heavy feet moving toward her through the underbrush. She turned her head. A dark brown, hump-backed bear was rising up on its haunches. It was huge.

It was looking directly at her.

She jumped to her feet and it charged at her, tromping quickly at first and then halting as it neared her. It stood again, over three feet taller than she, its mighty, lethal claws mere feet from her face. To Rebecca's terrified eyes the beast looked to be over a thousand pounds. Its coat gave off a gamy, greasy stench.

Rebecca eased the whip from around her waist and readied her arm for the strike.

"Father in heaven, if this is my time to go, don't let me suffer. Please."

On all fours now, the immense bear moved forward. Rebecca cracked the whip against its turned-up nose several times very quickly. The bear backed up. It shook its massive head and snarled fiercely, baring monstrous teeth. Rebecca felt her bones dissolve but continued to pop her whip, the handle damp in her sweaty palm.

The enraged brute rose up again, roaring, slashing, its small fiery eyes savage with fury. It lunged at her ferociously, swinging its gigantic front legs. Reaching for her.

From out of nowhere, an arrow sank deeply into the creature's chest. More arrows flew—from everywhere, it seemed to Rebecca—all aimed at the bear. The monster collapsed, dead.

From behind the trees, fewer than a dozen natives emerged, some returning unused arrows to their buckskin quivers. Trembling, she watched them come forward. Each man wore a deerskin shirt, leggings and moccasins. They pointed at her whip and spoke a language that was very familiar to her, but dissimilar in some ways.

"Who are you?" Rebecca asked in the Lakota tongue her father had taught her.

Hearing tribal language, they exchanged looks. A weathered, middle-aged brave put his fist to his chest.

"Big Thunder." He said, then pointed to two younger men, "My sons, Watching Owl and Little Bull. This *mato*, this bear, has caused trouble in our camp for many days. We were hunting for it."

"I'm grateful you were here," Rebecca said. She stood back on shaky legs and watched as the Indians said a prayer of thanksgiving to the bear for giving up its life. Then they skinned it. They whooped in happiness and teased each other as they cut the meat.

Rebecca was still standing there unsteadily, all agog, when Little Bull touched her arm and pointed at her whip.

"Long arm that bites," he said.

He was nut brown, with long black hair parted in the center and flowing past his shoulders. His almond-shaped eyes were friendly. Rebecca could see he was fascinated with her whip. She gathered it up and wrapped it around her waist again. Little Bull watched her intently with ebony eyes.

"Whip," Rebecca said as she pointed to the weapon wrapped around her.

"Long arm that bites," Little Bull repeated.

Rebecca lifted her hand in farewell and backed away, still shaking but smiling, thankful to be alive. Little Bull turned back to the others. The natives ignored her as she trudged off to find Buster.

Riding homeward, she felt a little queasy, but she considered herself lucky indeed. Her mind swirled with disturbing conjecture of the horrors that could have been.

* * *

She told no one of her harrowing encounter with the bear, or of her experience with the natives. The cattlemen were so busy with the spring roundup that they were hardly around. Martina's matchmaking campaign seemed to come to an end for Cooper as the calving season began.

The days became even warmer and the wild fruit trees bloomed. Gooseberry and chokecherry bushes and native plum trees grew near the stream where Rebecca's terrifying brush with danger had occurred. She knew she would return to reap their harvest, hazardous or not.

* * *

The air was still but for the bees buzzing around her and the scolding of birds from a nearby pine. Rebecca popped a handful of dark berries into her mouth, squeezed juice from them, and spit out the seeds and skin. The sweet fruit tasted luscious on her tongue. She looked to the ground for ripe, fallen berries and, curiously, a pair of moccasined feet were in her line of sight.

Her eyes ran a path from moccasins up long, well-developed legs to breechcloth, up and across bare brown torso to a striking face. When her eyes met his, he smiled. He pointed at her whip.

"Long Arm That Bites."

Rebecca smiled happily in return.

"Little Bull. Where are your people?"

He turned and arced his hand in a wide swoop.

"Not far." He began helping her fill her basket with fruit.

They picked berries in silence for a time. Then Little Bull spoke again, his voice low and pleasant.

"Whose woman is Long Arm That Bites?" He hesitantly touched the whip at her waist.

Rebecca glanced at him in surprise.

"Free maiden." The basket was full. Time for her to go. She saw that the Indian's intense black eyes were focused on her whip.

"Do you want to learn?" she asked as she began to uncoil it.

Little Bull's eyes lit up. She reached for his hand to place the swivel handle in his roughened palm. He didn't flinch and accepted her touch as if they were old friends. Rebecca allowed him to study the weapon, turning it over in his hands. Then he began to fling his arm about and to watch in fascination the writhing of the whip.

Rebecca laughed at his antics and grabbed his arm.

"Watch," she directed.

He allowed her to take the whip back and observed closely as she extended it to its fullest length beside her, stretched out behind.

"It magnifies your energy, your every move," she said, trying to find the right words for him to understand. "It builds up at the tip but you must direct the force."

She showed him that her grip was relaxed and flexible. In a smooth, gentle motion, she dragged her arm up and over. Again the whip was stretched at its full length, but now alongside and in front of her. She handed it back to him.

"You try, but don't hold it like a club."

Rebecca patiently continued the lesson until Little Bull had mastered the most basic movements. The sun was low when she finally said, "Must go."

She reached out for the whip and he gave it to her without hesitation. He remained where he was as she wreathed her waist with the whip. He lifted her basket of berries and handed them to her after she'd mounted Buster. Rebecca held up her forearm with palm flat, her fingers pointing heavenward, signing her thanks and good-bye. He reached out and placed his palm against hers.

"Do you want to learn more?"

He gave a brief nod.

"Meet me here in two suns. Can you do that?"

Little Bull made a guttural sound of agreement. Rebecca rode away with satisfaction in her heart. She had made another friend.

* * *

That evening she whistled as she helped Daisy in the kitchen.

The robust woman was tucking away the last two sugar cookies.

"Aren't you happy," she said to Rebecca, not as a question but a statement of fact.

"I made a new acquaintance today."

"Who could that have been? I don't recall any young ladies in these parts who'd be near the berry bushes."

Rebecca laughed blithely. "His name is Little Bull."

"An Indian!" Daisy said with dismay written on her plump face. "I don't think it wise for you to hang around with those savages, child, especially a brave."

The smile left Rebecca's face. Her bright mood had vanished.

"He means no harm. He treats me respectfully. He just wants to learn how to use my whip. What harm can come from that?"

"I don't think it's wise," Daisy repeated. "It will bring you trouble."

"Not if you don't tell anyone, it won't," Rebecca said.

"Hmmph." Daisy left the room without another word.

Rebecca watched her go and wondered if she would keep her secret.

* * *

Two days later she kept her promise and met Little Bull for another lesson. He learned quickly, sensitive to the feel of the tool, slicing through the air with a measure of competence.

"*Was té*," she said. "Good!" Together, they also picked more berries. "This is so no one questions where I've been, what I've been doing," she told him.

"Family would not like?" Little Bull pointed in the direction of the Conrad Ranch.

"They would not like," she repeated, amazed at his astuteness. She treasured the friendship of this clever, dusky-skinned man. She held up her hand to bid him farewell. Little Bull was about to place his hand on hers when they heard hoof beats nearby.

The Indian noiselessly ran for the cover of nearby trees, glancing over his shoulder in a silent plea for her to hide, too. It was too late. Rebecca had seen who had discovered her. She groaned, "Cooper."

She watched warily as he rode up, reining his gelding beside her. He dismounted instantly and gripped her shoulder roughly, pushing his flushed, twisted face into hers.

"What were you doing with an Indian buck?" he bellowed. His eyes were black and baleful.

"Nothing! Nothing *wrong!*" she insisted, squirming, trying to extricate herself from his grasp. Tears welled in her eyes, but she did not cry out.

Cooper released her then and glared down at her belligerently. "I'm not feeding any half-breeds, you got that?"

You already are, Rebecca thought cynically, *since I'm of mixed blood.*

"First you tempt our foreman, and now this heathen!"

His acid tone stung like fire. Rebecca couldn't reply to defend herself; it was all she could do to hold back a sob.

"Get home." His eyes were stormy and accusing, his voice sounded disheartened.

Rebecca mounted Buster, raked her heels on his sides and shot past Cooper. *How dare he make such degrading accusations?* she thought reproachfully. It was he who had the reputation of a philanderer. He didn't deserve an explanation.

* * *

Cooper had seen the Indian, who stepped from the shadows into plain sight and watched them coolly. *A handsome devil,* Cooper admitted to himself. *But what do I care?* Somehow he couldn't convince a part of him, deep inside, that he didn't.

That evening, when Rebecca brought a serving platter to the supper table, Cooper had an idea.

"Mother, I think my room is due for a thorough cleaning, top to bottom." He ventured a look at Rebel.

Rebecca straightened her back, eyes flaring.

"Oh?" Martina took note of the interplay between the two of them. "Why do you think that, Cooper?"

"I saw cobwebs in the corner and dust balls under my dresser."

His eyes never left Rebecca's. *It's not true, but it'll keep you too busy to meet that savage tomorrow,* he thought fiercely.

Martina's face held a curious expression. She looked at her son as if it were a miracle he'd be interested in anything to do with housekeeping. "I suppose your room must have been neglected, although I really haven't seen a speck of dust anywhere, dear. Rebecca can clean it tomorrow."

"See that she takes her time over it," Cooper said as he broke the hold he had on Rebel's eyes and looked at his mother instead.

* * *

Rebecca went through Cooper's room with infinite care, dusting and polishing and scouring until it was immaculate. There weren't any cobwebs or dust balls anywhere, as she'd known all along.

He lied, she steamed, *as a kind of punishment for me, or to keep me here, too busy to leave. Well, the joke's on him.* She wasn't going to see Little Bull that day anyway. They'd planned to meet again in two suns.

She had just finished folding Cooper's laundered underwear, fresh from the clothesline, and was about to replace it into newly-cleaned drawers when Cooper walked in. His magnetic eyes clashed with hers.

Rebecca was taken aback.

"I thought your mother had you safely cloistered away in the parlor with Carmella." She kept her voice light. Cooper was dressed more informally than courtship usually called for. His shirt collar was open. He wore his shirtsleeves rolled up, revealing tanned, muscular forearms. Tight denim pants encased his long, lean legs.

"I wanted a few minutes of peace. Used the excuse of needing a clean handkerchief. I must say it's nice to come to my room and see you playing with my underwear."

"Playing with . . . !" Flustered, Rebecca was unable to finish the sentence. She felt the heat of a blush ebb up her neck to her ears as if she were guilty of doing such a thing.

Cooper took a few steps toward her, flashing a devil-be-damned smile. He reached out and firmly but gently caught her chin.

"Only you and my Mama have touched my private clothes."

There was laughter in his sparkling chocolate eyes.

Rebecca opened her mouth and closed it again,

unable to find the words. Her mouth felt dry. She flicked her tongue out to wet her lips and it caught his attention. He drew in his breath quickly. She heard it! He raised her face to his, and she saw that his eyes were no longer laughing. They were hooded with emotion, an aching, a yearning. He flicked his tongue where hers had just been.

Heart racing, Rebecca gasped in surprise. Cooper covered her mouth with his and filled it with his questing tongue, sending sparks of fire flickering through her. Her lips yielded and she opened herself up for more. His demanding tongue probed deeper, making her knees go weak. Her arms stole around his shoulders as she found herself sagging into him.

His arm snug around her lower back, he pulled her tightly to him as her body began to sink. He cradled her head with his other hand, burying his fingers in her hair. His heartbeat thudded against her breast. Or was it her heart that thundered so? He tore his lips from hers and nestled her face into the harbor of his neck, breathing raggedly.

"Rebecca," he murmured hoarsely.

A moan escaped her as she reveled in the sensations crashing through her. The feel of his broad, muscular back under her fingers, his virile scent, the taste of him. Her senses were reeling. His hands found her buttocks and squeezed gently, then pulled her pelvis even closer. She felt his male hardness and arched into it, her breath heavy with desire.

"Cooper!" Martina screamed in outrage from the hallway. "What do you think you are doing?"

Chapter Eleven

"Cooper! I might have known I'd find you with her." Martina stood at the bedroom door, her face enveloped in antagonism. She stared at them with eyes as cold and hard as ebony marbles.

Cooper felt as if his flaming skin had been doused in ice water. Rebecca jerked out of his arms like a kitten on a hot stove. Her look of culpability, as if she were somehow terribly guilty, made him chuckle softly. Her eyes widened at his laughter.

The laughter went out of his eyes as he coolly looked at his mother.

"I came to get a clean handkerchief and thought I might advise Rebel on how to arrange the drawers."

Rebecca, whose attention had been firmly fixed on the incensed Martina, was startled into gaping at Cooper.

She's shocked by the silly little lie to my mother, he thought. He watched Rebecca put her palms to her reddened cheeks.

"Cooper, I want you in the parlor right now and on your best behavior," Martina commanded vehemently. Her exotic features were tarnished with suspicion and anger.

"I am not some kid, Mother." He narrowed his eyes and spaced his words meaningfully, "I am a grown man and I will choose with whom I sit in the parlor and how I will behave while doing it. I told you I will handle my life my way and in my time."

Martina stared at him for a long moment, her eyes filling with tears. When she turned stiffly to leave, Cooper relented and went to her.

"Mother," he crooned mournfully.

"That girl has been inveigling herself into your affections ever since, well, probably from before you brought her home." She faced him, stony-eyed. "She is an adventuress who has set her cap for you."

"That's not true, Mother. Rebel's an innocent. She's blameless."

"She's beguiled you, I'm sure of it. But she is expendable. I can replace her with another quite easily." Martina turned on her heel and left.

Cooper stood there clenching and unclenching his fists.

"Rebel, I'm so sorry."

Rebecca visibly struggled to regain her composure. With all his might Cooper willed her to look at him, but she didn't make eye contact. Within moments she seemed to recover her equilibrium. She left the room, head high.

* * *

He found her at the birdbath in the garden, her favorite place of green, leafy seclusion. She was sitting on the fieldstones, staring up at the statue. The creamy curve of her upturned throat was heartbreakingly beautiful to him.

When she turned her wide, intelligent eyes on him, he saw they'd changed. They held unyielding resolve in their liquid depths.

"I won't be made to feel ashamed, Cooper."

"I—I'm sorry, Rebel. I didn't mean to—and yesterday, too. I was distrusting. I shouldn't have said the things I did." He sat beside her. "I was worried about you out there with that savage. He might have kidnapped you, made you his woman! I didn't mean to sound so hateful. I would never want to hurt you."

I was covetous. I was jealous, he realized with wonder.

He was close enough to smell the delicate fragrance of her hair. He wanted more than anything to gather her up and experience her sweet taste again.

She lowered translucent, pearly eyelids.

"What do you want from life, Coop? Do you have hopes and dreams for the future?"

The sun had disappeared under a gloomy mantle; with the threat of rain, the idyllic garden seemed dreary. But Cooper felt sheltered with Rebel at his side. He gave her all his attention.

"I want to meet my obligations to my family. I want to improve this ranch. The land needs to be managed properly and I aim to do it. I have a lot of ideas for the future."

Rebecca shot him a clear-eyed look and arched one well-defined brow.

"Your mother is determined that you marry soon."

Thunder boomed in the distance.

He stiffened.

No woman will ever hold my heart hostage!

"Women are like fine horses to me." he said, "I can appreciate them, but I wouldn't want to be hitched to the same one forever. I harbor no illusions about wedded bliss, believe me." He clenched the muscles of his jaw. "Wives become shrews. My father was a push-over, hen-pecked to death. I goaded him to be more of a man, but—"

"It's a sad house where the hen crows loudest." She fixed him with her large green eyes. "You're not your father." The purposeful look came over her face again, and she said, "About your mother, tell her for me that I appreciate the roof over my head, the good food in my belly, the friends I've made here in the last year."

Rebecca wants to appease her. My mother should be the one doing the placating, Cooper thought.

"You know, Reb, I admire the way you do what you feel you have to do. You showed real gumption on the way here from Dakota. You took the heat and the dust and the hardship without a complaint. You're the most courageous woman I know."

"All is not butter that comes from the cow." Her rosy lips curled up at one corner, and her eyes glimmered at her own quip.

She bent her head and Cooper yearned to feel once again the shiny, smooth tresses slipping through his fingers. The plain brown dress she wore would have been homely on anyone else. On her, it brought out the toffee and caramel streaks in her brown hair. And with her slender curves filling it.

She looked away, into the past.

"When we came here, Coop, you were so grouchy on the trail, fuming about our slowness. I didn't much care for that side of you. But you were just concerned. I do understand."

They'd never spoken so intimately before. It made him feel wondrous inside. It warmed him even as he smelled cold rain hovering in threatening clouds.

* * *

Rebecca raced to her room and began throwing her meager things together. She tossed clothing and her Bible into an old saddlebag; she lifted the mattress and snatched up her money.

Daisy came in after her, running a fretful hand through her mouse-gray hair.

"What are you doing? Where are you going?"

Rebecca changed quickly into her father's old clothes. "I should never have come here in the first place," she told her. She hugged the buxom woman and said, gently, "You've been very kind to me and I'll always remember that. Chester and Blackie are good friends, too. Will you tell them I'll miss them, too? I didn't get to say goodbye to Chalina or Yago, either. Please, tell them I'm sorry."

Daisy fluttered worriedly. "But it's late in the day, it's going to rain. Don't do this now."

"I'm taking the horse," Rebecca told her resolutely. "Cooper once told me Buster is mine to keep, but I'll find a way to return him to the ranch. Promise me," she said with force, "Promise you won't let them hurt Madam."

"Cooper wouldn't allow anyone to harm that cow, you know that."

"She was a g-gift from my parents," Rebecca said, close to crying. "When I married someday, the selling of Madam's offspring was to help furnish a new home."

"Don't you worry about Madam, dear." Daisy wrung her hands anxiously. "Rebel, you're not the type to run away from a challenge—"

"Maybe not, but I *am* the type to leave when it's time to go."

Rebecca made for the door, wrapping the serpentine coils of her whip around her waist.

Martina blocked the exit, her eyes black mirrors of anger.

"I have made Carmella's father a loan, a dowry of sorts, to ensure the hand of his daughter in marriage to my son. *Nothing* will prevent their wedding, you understand?"

Rebecca brushed past her, saying nothing.

* * *

She found Micah at the corrals, as she'd known she would. In the past year he hadn't filled out much, and the freckles that made their way over his nose and cheeks still gave him the look of youth.

"Rebel!" He smiled, eyeing her clothes and the saddlebag she carried. "Surely you're not going riding with a thunderstorm coming." He raised his head to the blackening sky and wrinkled his short, wide nose at it.

"Don't worry about me, I can take care of myself. Micah, I mean it," she said, looking directly into his golden eyes, "I know that's what friends do, care about each other, but I'll be all right."

She ruffled his wheat-colored hair affectionately, turned and walked away as the first, fat droplets splattered from the sky.

* * *

She nudged Buster into a lope, a rhythm accented by crashing thunderclaps and frightful flashes of lightning. As they splashed along, she examined the past year. Her future self would avoid past mistakes. Her tomorrows were blank pages on which she could write a new life. Again.

Martina hadn't been too far from the truth. She'd recognized Rebecca's lovesick yearnings. Cooper's nearness had tormented her the entire year. Now that she knew the euphoria of his touch, his mouth, his body so close to hers, it would damn near kill her to not be near him. Leaving was best. While she still had a shred of pride left.

I felt so secure in his arms, so treasured.

Rebecca's hot tears merged with the cold rain on her cheeks; the downpour reminded her of the twister that had torn her farm apart. It was fate that brought the two Conrad boys to her cellar that day. It was meant to be.

She had followed her heart, relinquishing her hopes of keeping her father's dream alive. On the trail, she had killed the snake that had threatened Cooper. He had handled another kind of snake who'd menaced her. *Norm.*

She pushed Kearn from her mind and thought fondly of the many friends she'd made at the ranch. *I'm not the same belittled farm girl I was, wearing old work clothes until they were rags.*

She'd grown accustomed to petticoats and nice things, warm lodgings and all the roast beef she could eat. She remembered Cooper's kindnesses, sweet moments that had touched her with his thoughtfulness. Perhaps he was a bounder, Rebecca thought ruefully. He was also a gentleman. A gentleman who would surely wed a genteel, polished "lady" as his overbearing mother was contriving for him to do.

The rain slowed to a light patter, then to a few drips and then it stopped. The earthy smell of wet horse wafted about her. She'd meet Little Bull tomorrow, as they'd planned, but first she'd spend a cold, damp night alone under the pines.

* * *

She hadn't slept well, chilled and wet, and she was weary to the bone when Little Bull arrived. He seemed to know things were different for her; his noble bronzed face showed concern. But he proudly showed her the whip he'd made of braided buffalo hide, and told her he'd practiced with it for many hours.

"I go with my people toward the north now," he said, his eyes as black as newly-turned earth. "The Great Father, your president, treats us as children, and we are becoming more angry. White men have come into our land as a swarm of insects, killing the buffalo of the Teton people. We go north."

Rebecca looked into his brown face and saw her own sadness reflected there. She remembered the paltry cluster of bison Cooper had pointed out to her on their trek westward. The Laramie Treaty of '68 had been broken by hordes of whites who built roads and destroyed hunting grounds. "I, too, must leave this area," she said.

"I can show you how to reach a settlement that is south-west, about two suns from here." He picked up a stick and drew directions in the soil. He sketched symbols representing landmarks, explaining them to Rebecca.

What will I do once I find it? she asked herself. Sadly she watched her friend depart, knowing she might never see him again.

She studied the drawing in the dirt, memorizing it. When she could close her eyes and recall the drawing perfectly, she destroyed it and rode away.

Chapter Twelve

At a deeply forested rise overlooking the settlement of Promise, Rebecca paused and felt a newborn excitement, a lighter, happier heart.

She hid behind a tree and changed into the plain green dress, crumpled but clean. She stashed her whip in the saddle bag, mounted, and arranged her dress properly. Then she took a deep breath and cued Buster to walk sedately.

The path became a rutted street between a cluster of false-fronted pine buildings, some newer and taller than others. Rebecca saw canvas tents, too, and sheds, and a lean-to. She heard a door squeak and saw a balding man come out on the boardwalk before the general store. He was carrying a broom, and began sweeping the walkway in front of the establishment.

"Good morning, sir." Rebecca dismounted a mere three feet from him. He stopped his work and stood there, watching her.

"Afternoon," he said, and began to sweep again.

"My name is Rebecca LaRoche. I'm wondering if there might be any work for a decent woman in this settlement?"

"Might be. Where ya from?"

"Yankton, Dakota Territory."

"Kinda strange, a young gal like you travelin' that distance alone," he said.

"I came from Yankton a year ago to be a housemaid to a family near the Bearlodge Mountains. The lady of the house thought I was wanting one of her sons and took umbrage with me, so I left."

"Well, did ya? Want one of her sons?" The man winked.

"No!" Rebecca was surprised at the intimate question from a stranger.

"Weren't using your head then, missy," he said, shaking his head as if he were a schoolteacher giving a bad mark to a student. He pointed his chin at a two-story building across the way. "You might ask Tillie if she could use ya."

Rebecca turned around to survey Tillie's. A sign above the door read, simply, The Inn. The storekeeper cleared his throat and she faced him again.

"Or, you might try one of the saloons, if ya have to. If that be, then they're up the lane a ways." He jerked his head to the side. Raucous laughter and music emanated from that end of town. Men moved in and out of three buildings there as if in a rhythm.

"No, thank you. I'll try Tillie's."

"Yes, ma'am. Chances are good she needs your help. Plenty of men around these parts got no wives to do their cookin' for 'em. Might be you'll find a man right quick, too."

Just let that comment pass, Rebecca cautioned herself. She settled Buster in at the livery stable and headed for the café, stomach growling.

She entered to the tinkle of a little bell that was fastened to the door. The enticing aroma of good food filled the air. Rebecca stopped and examined the room, empty of people. She counted half a dozen square tables that could seat four people each. All were covered with the same patterned cloth. The tables, cut crudely from logs, looked very primitive compared to Mrs. Conrad's fine imported furniture.

A thin, middle-aged woman came out of a back room, drying red, chapped hands on a pinafore made of the same material as the tablecloths.

"May I get you something? The noon meal was beef roast, but I've no meat left. I've got a smidgen of potatoes and gravy, but no pie, either."

"The potatoes will be fine, thank you," Rebecca replied as she headed for the nearest table. She wondered how she would broach the subject of work to the woman. She'd disappeared into the back room again, and Rebecca heard the tinny sounds of banging and scraping.

The woman poked her head through the doorway.

"Would you like a cup of coffee as you wait?" She pointedly looked at the windows up front, as if to see whether Rebecca would be joined by anyone.

"Yes, that would be nice. I'm here alone, by the way."

"No! A little bitty thing like you? What on earth are you doing in these parts by yourself?"

"Well, ma'am, I'm looking for a position. I've come from a ranch northeast of here, where I worked for my board and room."

"Why didn't you stay there, where you could be safe, girl?"

Rebecca cleared her throat. It was embarrassing to admit she'd been too proud to stay. It made her look as if she were not a dependable worker.

"The lady of the house thought I was trying to marry into the family. It wasn't true!"

"Bit of a snoot, was she?" The kind-faced, pewter-haired lady laughed. "Well, you got yourself a job, gal, and I'll even give you wages. I'm Tillie."

"Thank you! My name is Rebecca, by the way,

Rebecca LaRoche. I can start immediately." Rebecca was delighted.

Tillie laughed heartily and patted Rebecca on the shoulder.

"You just sit and eat first, dear. I think I'm gonna like having you around to save my poor old legs and feet." She left to check on the potatoes and Rebecca raised a silent prayer.

Tillie returned with a steamy plate of mashed potatoes with brown gravy mixed in. Rebecca ate ravenously.

"A mite hungry, were you? When you're finished, bring your plate and cup back and we'll get you busy."

"Yes ma'am!" Rebecca said, excited and impatient to start her new work.

Tillie showed Rebecca how to ready the tables, and together they prepared for the hungry men who would inundate them at the supper hour.

Rebecca soon learned to wait on customers, to take orders, to deliver several plates at once to tables—the myriad skills a waitress must possess. Within a week she'd become Tillie's right hand and had made several new friends.

The male customers teased her mercilessly, often becoming physical, touching her hand or pinching her bottom. At first their familiarity bothered Rebecca, but finally she understood that the men did it in fun. They didn't mean to be insulting. Rebecca learned, by Tillie's example, how to flirt harmlessly back.

One afternoon, after she'd become very good at the thrust and parry of words, she realized, *I'm just like Liza and Jezreel! These men want my attention, and I lead them on.* A strange, new sense of power, of *arrival,* came over her at that moment.

Under Tillie's tutelage in the kitchen, Rebecca soon expanded her repertoire of dishes, and she learned how to cook in quantity. She found the work satisfying.

Though she'd helped in the Conrad kitchen, it had been Daisy's little kingdom.

"'Round here," Tillie said, "it don't matter much how the grub looks, or even how it tastes, so long as there's plenty of it." The twinkle in her eyes betrayed her poker face.

The kitchen was neat and clean, but small. Two of the walls were covered with pots of all sizes hanging on ten penny nails. To Rebecca it seemed an abundance of pans. In one corner sat barrels of smoked meats and pickled vegetables, stout cloth sacks of flour and sugar, and crates of eggs. A trap door in the floor led to the root cellar.

To work with such a profusion of supplies was a pleasure, Rebecca thought. Tins of spices neatly lined one shelf. A wooden table held a mixing bowl, rolling pin, and sifter, waiting to make something doughy. Tillie's one extravagance was the large cook stove, new and shiny with chrome. When fired up, it would warm the room cozily in winter, but it would give off unbearable heat during the worst days of summer. Next to the back door, a pile of wood waited to stoke the stove.

One unseasonably hot September morning, as the two women sat peeling potatoes together in companionable silence, Rebecca's thoughts turned to Cooper and his supercilious mother, as they often did.

"I'd give anything to know what's going on at the Conrad household right about now," she said pensively.

"Did you say 'Conrad?'" Tillie stared at her, two spots of red appearing high on her pale cheeks. "I'll venture to guess the lady of that house is the uppity Martina Conrad."

Rebecca looked at her with raised brows. "Do you know her?"

"Yep. Had a bit of a run-in with her a long time ago.

We were after the same man . . . I just about had him, too, before she moved in with her rich Spanish folks . . . and that was the end of it. He flew over the moon in love with her. I've never wanted another man since."

"I'm sorry to hear that." Rebecca patted the older woman's thin, care-worn hand. "I've often wondered how Mrs. Conrad could have such a princely home when the area hasn't been opened up all that long. I was seven years old when my mother and father started homesteading, and our property never reached such opulence as Mrs. Conrad's."

"Large amounts of her family's money backed it up at the start," Tillie said. She took a large breath and expelled it slowly, as if wondering how much to tell Rebecca.

"Years back, California belonged to the Spanish," she recounted. "An Italian-American came from the East—he would become Martina Conrad's father eventually—and fell deeply in love with a beautiful Spanish girl.

"That would be Martina's mother?" Rebecca interrupted.

"Yes, the Spanish beauty would become Martina's mother. It was difficult for the Italian, though, because the girl's father was a wealthy, powerful man, one of the Spanish Dons that had settled the area earlier. And he only had the one daughter, of whom he was very protective. But the Italian ingratiated himself into the Don's trust. He was a hard worker, he was unfailingly honest, and he made himself indispensable."

"All that money and a lovely woman besides," mused Rebecca as she thought of the qualities Cooper shared with his Italian forebear.

"The daughter loved her suitor in return, and the Don allowed them to marry. They had a pretty daughter, Martina, and spoiled her dreadfully."

"How did Martina meet Mr. Conrad?"

"Mr. Conrad—Luke—was a big, beautiful man with waves of thick blond hair." Tillie's eyes focused on the past. "His mother grew up in California, where her parents raised grapes. She met a shopkeeper named Conrad, ran off and married him without her parents' blessing, and was disowned. The young couple eked out a living and slowly gained a foothold in society. They had a handsome, big-boned son . . . Luke. He was something!"

Rebecca saw the stars light up in Tillie's faraway gaze and knew she'd cherished Luke Conrad.

"You really loved him, didn't you?"

"I adored him," Tillie whispered. There was a moment of reflective silence before she continued. "My father caught the gold rush fever a little late, unfortunately. By the time he dragged our family over the prairies in a wagon train, what gold there was in California had already been claimed. He went looking for honest work to support us and found it in Conrad's Mercantile.

"Luke and I grew up together. We talked of marriage. Both our families expected us to wed. When he pushed for something more than a kiss, I knew I'd be his soon anyway." Tillie stared at the half-peeled potato in her hand, surely not seeing it.

She still hadn't explained how Luke had met Martina. Rebecca sat quietly, hoping the tale wouldn't end now, but feeling it would be utterly rude on her part to push for more.

"Hmm," Tillie sighed. "One day a black-haired beauty walked into the store and we all stood in awe. She reeked of money and power. Luke gaped at her worshipfully and I knew at that moment I'd lost him. My only hope was that she wouldn't return his regard, but would snub him instead. When he stepped boldly forward and offered to help her, my hopes were dashed. She flirted with him outrageously." She rubbed at her eyes with both veiny hands.

"Oh, Luke and I still talked after that—but only as *friends.*" She hissed the last word and made a sour face. "He loved telling me the romantic story of Martina's parents, almost as much as I hated hearing it! He married her rather quickly and then heard of gold being found up this way. They joined a wagon train and came to these parts, started the ranch . . . ."

Tillie's voice trailed off again, and this time her story-telling was done. Still, her distant eyes told of haunting memories being replayed.

* * *

Rebecca was alone in the kitchen, scrubbing carrots, when a knock came at the back door. She hesitated a moment and a baritone voice shouted, "Tillie!"

"She's running an errand, she's not here."

A tall, sandy-haired man entered. He had an olive complexion and coffee-brown eyes that flickered brightly, like the metal studs on his jersey shirt. He was broad in the shoulders and narrow of hip. He stepped closer, and Rebecca saw that his facial skin was fine and soft-looking, covered with pale, fine peach-fuzz.

"Hello! And who are you?" He spoke with a brogue Rebecca found fascinating, and he smiled at her with full, lush lips.

"Rebecca. I'm helping Tillie."

"Becky, is it?"

Rebecca nodded agreeably, still too occupied with his beige and brown coloring—and his wonderful accent—to realize he'd shortened her name. When it finally hit her, it was too late to repudiate it. At least his nickname for her was better than "Rebel" or "Reb," she told herself. Far better.

"Is Tillie around?"

"Ahhh, yes," she murmured absently, and then realized what she'd said. "I mean no!" The wet carrot she'd been grasping slipped out of her nervous hand and was deftly caught by the man who reminded her of peaches, or maybe coffee with milk.

He chuckled as he saw the red heat rise from Rebecca's neck to her ears.

"Excitable little root, isn't it," he said as he handed the wayward carrot back to her. All Rebecca could do was nod.

"Well, Virgil, I hope this means you've brought me some beef?" asked Tillie as she entered the room.

"Yes, indeed it does, and it's all cut up for you as well." He winked at Rebecca, turned and held the back door open for Tillie to pass through again to the outdoors. A few minutes later Tillie returned and opened the cellar door.

Virgil followed, carrying a full gunny sack that smelled of raw meat. He disappeared down the cellar with it, then repeated the same routine several times over until Tillie's order was complete.

"What do I owe you this time?" asked Tillie

"I'll put the price down to half the usual, if I can steal Becky away to go fishing on Sunday afternoon," Virgil said.

"Now, what would your daddy say to that?" questioned Tillie.

"Daddy doesn't have to know."

"Oh, go on, you young pup. Get outta here!" Tillie said with a swipe at his firm derriere.

Virgil chuckled as he dodged Tillie's swat. "See you Sunday, Becky girl," he said as he slipped through the back door.

It's my choice whether you will or won't, Rebecca thought.

"That boy is gonna get himself into a heap of trouble with his daddy if he carries on with you."

"Why is that?" Rebecca asked.

"Virgil's father has a girl all picked out for him back home in Scotland. He gets wind of Virgil's interest in someone else, he's gonna ship that boy over there pronto."

"Going fishing together seems pretty harmless, Tillie. Are you going to tell?"

"Me? Oh, no. No, I'll let the boy have fun, but I warn you, don't go gettin' yourself in the family way by him. He's not for you."

Rebecca was taken aback. Suddenly the subject had gone from harmless fun to wanton ways.

Tillie's pale face took on the distant look that told Rebecca she was revisiting her past again. She began to speak, so softly that Rebecca strained to hear. "Twenty-six years ago, I—I found myself pregnant with Luke's child. I didn't tell him. I was young, too proud, too afraid. But I couldn't stay home and let my parents—or his—see me grow large with child.

"After he married and left with a wagon train, I ran away from home and joined another train coming this way. I guess I just had to follow him." She combed through her iron-gray hair with thin fingers, and smiled weakly at Rebecca. "I had the baby. Luke never knew. I gave him away to a childless couple that befriended me on the way here. Their names were Marcia and Floyd Dunn. They named my baby David."

Rebecca gasped in recognition of the name.

Chapter Thirteen

"You know my son?" Tillie asked.

Rebecca looked into the older woman's eyes with empathy. "Yes. He is a good lawyer, I hear. You should be very proud of him."

"I am. I've seen him a few times over the years. His adoptive parents told him about me when he became older. One day he showed up on my doorstep demanding I tell him who his real father was. I shouldn't have, but a devil sat on my shoulder that day."

"You told him! Oh, my!" Rebecca said. Now David's animosity toward Cooper made sense to her. "Unknowingly, Luke went to David—his own son—to have his will drawn up."

Tillie raised her eyebrows at that. "I see. That big ranch, and David thinking he should have part of it, as the eldest son." She put her hand to her forehead dazedly. "My poor baby. I need to tell him all that wealth came from Martina's side and not his father's." She went immediately for pen and paper to write him a letter. She addressed the envelope to his office in Gaspar.

Rebecca shook her head in amazement. "Now that I

know, the family resemblance is staggering. I can't believe no one else sees it." Suddenly her mind leaped to another thought. Maybe Martina realized the truth, and she was afraid Cooper would sire an illegitimate child, as his father had done. Maybe that's why she pushed him so mercilessly to marry.

Tillie sealed the envelope. "I'll be right back. I need to get this out with the next mail wagon."

"Tillie? Did Luke know you were here?"

"Yes and no. He bumped into me once, as I was coming off the stagecoach. I told him I had just arrived, but that I was continuing on to somewhere else. He never asked me where I was going, and I never told him."

Tillie left with her letter. Rebecca firmly told herself none of it was her concern and she should forget all about it. The Conrads were out of her life forever.

* * *

Tillie had given Rebecca a spacious, light-filled corner room on the second floor to call her own. Braided rugs and lacy white crocheted curtains added a feminine touch. Rebecca luxuriated in her ample living quarters, so much more pleasant than her cramped space at the Conrad's.

Although Cooper intruded into her mind far too often, Rebecca also enjoyed the people who frequented the Inn. She noticed a pattern in some of the daily customers' habits. One of the regulars was a silver-haired gentleman everyone simply called Judge. He would come in shortly after the dinner hour with a pile of papers. He'd order a cup of coffee and begin to read. Rebecca would see that his cup was always filled. In another hour a handsome, well-dressed woman, Angela, the Judge's wife, always would join him. They appeared to be very good friends with Virgil, who often sat with them for a time.

"Becky, you will come fishing with me this Sunday."

"Why, Virgil McCormick, have you made up your mind to come calling on me?" teased Rebecca

"I have."

"What about your daddy?"

"What he don't know won't hurt him," Virgil said as he grabbed Rebecca's arm and pulled her onto his lap.

Rebecca looked deep into his eyes to see what his real thoughts were, but all she saw was that mischievous twinkle that gave away nothing of his true feelings. "All right, I'll meet you here with a picnic basket," she said lightly. Tillie's warning still rang in her ears. *He's not for you.*

On Sunday Virgil stood by his carriage, looking dashing and gallant. He placed the picnic basket in the back with his fishing gear. *He's everything a woman could desire*, Rebecca thought, *so why am I so ambivalent? Do I want him as more than a friend?* "

"I've never fished for trout before," she told him as he gathered the reins.

"Then I'll teach you." There was a long silence except for the hypnotizing clopping of hooves and the whirring of buggy wheels. "Tell me about yourself," Virgil said, breaking the spell with his Scottish burr.

He listened avidly as she talked, but also stopped her at times to ask questions. No one, other than her parents, had been that attentive before. She thrived under it. Before Rebecca knew it, they had traveled several miles to a turbulent, fast-moving creek and Virgil was handing her down from the carriage.

He began teaching her the fine points of fly fishing by opening a small wooden box filled with many hooks decorated with hair and feathers. He placed one on the end of his fishing line, rolled up his pants legs, and stepped out into the churning water up to his knees.

He unwound a length of line and cast it in.

Rebecca watched attentively for a few minutes. When Virgil didn't return to the stony shore, she removed her shoes and stockings, took a pole and one of the prettier hooks, and waded out to him. The pebbles under her naked feet felt surprisingly smooth. Her skirts became wet and tangled around her legs and ankles in the rushing, foamy water.

"I should have known better than to come out here wearing a dress."

Virgil shot her a mischievous look. "You should probably remove those skirts later to let them dry. I like the idea of seeing you in only your bloomers."

"Shame on you, Virgil. You shouldn't know anything about bloomers."

He chuckled and came to stand behind her. He placed his arms around her to help her toss her line. The close contact with him felt good; it made her want to lean back against him. The cold mountain water on her legs went unnoticed.

"Becky, you have a bite. All good things must come to an end," he whispered into her ear. He breathed in as if taking in her scent.

Together they wrestled the silvery, iridescent fish in and Virgil carried it to shore, Rebecca following him. "I'm a bit hungry. What about you, Becky?" he asked as he placed the fish in a hamper.

"Mm-hmm."

They sat together under a tree and nibbled away on turkey legs. Virgil placed his arm around Rebecca, drawing her closer to him. She rested her cheek on his shoulder.

"You know I care for you, don't you, Becky?"

She turned to look into his eyes. He lowered his head and brought his sensuous, full lips to hers, kissing her gently.

Conflicted feelings clashed inside her. A frown

creased her brow and she pulled away, shaking her head.

"Let's get back to fishing," Virgil said as he jumped up abruptly and moved to pick up his line. Rebecca joined him in the water, but this time they stood a distance apart.

* * *

On the following Sunday Virgil returned to take her for a carriage ride. After many miles, he steered the horse to a hilltop near his home. The ranch was nestled in a valley below them, surrounded by trees. The sun had long since disappeared behind cloud cover; the sound of thunder drove down upon the two of them as they sat there.

Virgil cleared his throat and spoke over the noise. "We raise Hereford cattle. We get our stock from the Conrad ranch where you used to work."

Rebecca looked at him in surprise. Her heart thudded and she hungered to ask, *Have you spoken to Cooper about me? Does he know where I am?* But all she said was, "You know them, then?"

"Yes. The Conrads were the first in the area to have the breed. They are hardy cattle that can withstand the harsh conditions of these parts. The Hereford breed was imported from England by Henry Clay in Kentucky. The Conrads started their herd from him and my father's herd was begun from Conrad's.

"Your ranch looks to be as large as theirs."

"Yes, it is, but my father also dabbles in other things. He's an investor and has businesses in Europe as well as here in America." Virgil stared at his lap, suddenly reticent. Then he went on. "My father's the third son of a Scottish laird—he came here to settle against his father's wishes. He made several promises that need to be kept in order for peace to remain in the family.

"Have you been to Europe?"

"No, but I must go there soon. It was one of the promises— that my father's sons must visit the clan.

"Does one of the promises deal with your marriage?" asked Rebecca tentatively.

Virgil looked at her in surprise. "Yes, it does. How did you know?

"Tillie told me. Rather, I should say she *warned* me."

"I see. The Judge has been telling me I should travel to Scotland to see my betrothed. He seems to think it would be the fair thing to do."

Rebecca said softly, "Is that what you're going to do?"

"I'd rather not."

The thunder grew louder, driving them homeward, and a strong wind began to dance through the tree-tops. Virgil dropped her off at the back door with another sweet kiss.

* * *

Throughout the cooling fall Rebecca had discovered more and more about her own feminine vitality. She admired many qualities of the Judge's wife, Angela Covell; the stately woman had become a good friend. Rebecca saved her earnings and, with Angela's help, she learned to dress in fashion. She bought herself a topaz brooch, her first and only fine piece of jewelry. The faceted amber stone was surrounded by delicate seed pearls, and it looked pretty pinned at the high neckline of her new gold velvet gown.

Rebecca treated herself to silken underwear, too, lace-edged and beribboned. Even her hair underwent changes. Angela and Tillie worked with her until she could fashion her coiffure into a number of becoming styles.

By Christmas she had become the belle of Promise; men flocked to the Inn just to ignite her sparks. They were captivated, Angela said, by Rebecca's joviality, her patience, and her wit. The winter months passed quickly. Rebecca spent her afternoons and evenings in the fond company of Virgil, the Covells, and Tillie. Now and then, though, she felt again the loss of her farm, and she missed her friends from the ranch. Most troublesome of all, she couldn't seem to forget Cooper.

* * *

By early 1876, the gold rush Daisy had prophesied had come true. A frenzy of prospectors poured into the northern Black Hills. Placer claims were located on nearly every creek. Panning for gold had become the primary topic of conversation at the Inn.

One day in March Virgil entered with two men Rebecca didn't recognize. They huddled at a corner table, talking together enthusiastically.

"Becky, these are friends of mine," he said, gesturing around the table, "and we've decided to put some money together to search for gold ourselves."

"You and everyone else," Rebecca said with misgivings.

"Ah, but we'll be investigating the possibility of quartz lode claims, my dear. The mining of gold ore from the ledges." He sounded supremely confident.

"I have money saved I could put in the kitty."

A chuckle went around the table. "Women don't get involved with men's business," the ruddy-faced friend said.

"No, wait," the immense blue-eyed blonde put in, "money is money and we need it, no matter if it comes from a skirt or not."

All the men shrugged their shoulders. "I'll handle Becky's share," Virgil said.

She overheard bits and pieces of their conversation as she brought food and coffee to their table. When they were ready for Tillie's wild-cherry pie, she heard them talking about mules, shafts and mills.

Later, Rebecca sat alone with Virgil. "Can you trust these men?" she whispered in his ear.

"Yes, Broderick is like my second Pa and big Angus could be my brother. They are clansmen and came with us from Scotland. Don't worry, this will be a profitable venture, I'm sure of it."

"All right, if you say so."

Rebecca later told the Judge what she had done with every penny of her savings.

"I think your investment is safe with Virgil." he said, "I put some of my own money in, too."

* * *

Virgil returned to Promise on the first of April, with news that his partners were very close to discovering an outcrop of ore. He sat with Rebecca in the kitchen and entertained her with mining stories that made her laugh.

"That mule bucked and kicked to high heaven and Angus just hung on real tight. He made the funniest face, all eyes and round mouth, and his legs out straight and his big body bouncing all over!"

Rebecca looked at him warmly for a long, silent moment. Virgil abruptly stood and pulled her to her feet, tight against his rugged form. He fit his hand to the back of her head and kissed her with energy and need.

"We shouldn't be doing this," she said as she broke his hold on her. "I—I have great affection for you, Virgil, bu—"

He shook his head and interrupted her. "I think it's time I went to Scotland," he said quietly. "I have to settle things once and for all."

Rebecca kept her own countenance.

Virgil left the next day. Within two months he would meet the young lady to whom he was promised.

* * *

In the simmering heat of mid-summer Rebecca received a letter:

Dear Becky;

Forgive me. I met Colleen. She is beautiful beyond words and quite agreeable. I feel it would suit me better to follow my father's wishes.

Your investment is secure in Angus' hands. You will always have a very special place in my heart.

Virgil

Rebecca sat on the back step and peered unseeing at the sun-baked vista. She felt as shriveled inside as the scorched landscape, but she knew her melancholy was not for Virgil. She'd enjoyed his company, but she hadn't been in love with him. Her heart ached so. *Oh, Cooper, what are you doing right now, this moment?*

* * *

"Chalina, I don't know what to do with your oldest brother," wailed Martina. "Do you know what I've heard *now*?" She paced the parlor at full tilt, a handkerchief to her mouth.

Chalina stiffened. She knew what her mother was going to say. "I . . . I . . ." She shook her head, shrugged her shoulders and threw her hands out in front of her, palms up.

"Cooper has been spending all his free time at the brothel in town, with some horrid creature called

Fanny." Tears pooled in Martina's eyes. She dabbed at them with her lacy hankie. "My negotiations for a wedding to Carmella have come to naught. I give up!"

"Oh, Mama," Chalina said, trying to disguise her impatience. She put her arms around Martina and held her.

"He hears nothing I have to say—absolutely nothing."

Chalina led her mother to her favorite overstuffed chair.

"Let me see what Yago knows about all of this," she said in a mollifying tone.

She found Yago in the horse barn, grooming his stallion.

"Chalina. What brings you out of the house?"

"Mama. She's worried about Cooper and that loose woman, Fanny."

"So she's gotten wind of that, has she?"

Chalina nodded. "She's beside herself with worry. Can't we do something? Cooper's as touchy as an old bear, and he's about to lose his inheritance."

"He's in town right now, probably at the saloon. I'll talk with him when he comes home." Yago lifted one of the horse's feet and checked the pastern.

"You aren't the one sitting in the house with a weepy mother. I'm willing to go into town myself just to get clear of her complaining for a while."

"I won't hear of it. I'll go myself. Let me tell Millicent what I'm up to, and I'll be on my way. I have an idea."

"Can you tell me?" Chalina's dark eyes became animated.

"Coop's last hope may be to see the circuit judge. Maybe something can be done about that stipulation without his having to marry anyone."

"Oh, Yago, I hope so!" Chalina clapped her hands and turned to run back to the house.

* * *

Yago located Cooper nursing a severe hangover at Gaspar's only drinking establishment. "You're fast becoming the town drunk," he scolded, half in earnest.

Cooper's thick, black hair was mussed, his cheeks and chin were dark with stubble. His eyes were dark with troubled thoughts.

"No, little brother, the town drunk is Norm Kearn. I heard he was living with Marie over there." He nodded in the direction of a slovenly woman behind the bar. "I suppose Mother sent you in to get me."

"No, actually it was Chalina, but I've been meaning to talk with you. I have a feeling some of this behavior comes from that blasted stipulation."

Cooper faked a laugh. "Really, Yago, don't be ridiculous."

Yago's face remained stoic, stolid. "I have an idea."

"If you've come to offer up your idea of the ideal woman for me, forget opening your mouth."

"It's too late for a proper wedding," Yago said. "I thought we'd ride to Promise, see if the circuit judge can do something about that proviso. I brought along a copy of the will."

Cooper looked up with a glimmer of hope in his eyes. "You may have something there, James." He slapped Yago on the back. "Let's go."

They sent word back to the ranch and then began their ride. They arrived in Promise on the second day and stopped a cowboy on the street, asking for directions.

Yago pressed his horse into a canter through the dusty main street and pulled to a sliding stop in front of a private two-story house, with Cooper fast at his heels.

"Cross your fingers, big brother," Yago said. At the

front door he slammed the shiny knocker down. An elegant gray-haired woman ushered them into the judge's office and closed the door behind them for privacy.

The judge, bearded and mustachioed, sat regally behind his large walnut desk. He bowed his silver-thatched head at them as they entered.

"Thanks for seeing us, sir," Cooper said, and introduced his brother and himself.

Behind the judge's round spectacle lenses, a spark of recognition flickered at mention of the Conrad name. "Adam Covell, but just call me Judge, boys."

Yago held out the papers and pointed to the terms. "Can you do something about this?"

The Judge took the document and adjusted his wire earpieces. He read in silence while the brothers took seats before him. Cooper had crossed and uncrossed his long limbs for the twentieth time when the Judge finally cleared his throat. "It appears you have lost your land, young man, unless you have a girl ready to be married within the next two weeks."

Yago threw Cooper a sympathetic look.

"Sir, are you absolutely sure?" Cooper asked, sounding hopelessly discouraged.

"This is a very tightly drawn will." The Judge handed the papers to Cooper. "David Dunn is a good young lawyer. He knows what he's doing."

"He may be all that," Cooper said, "but he seems to have something against me for some reason. Ever since we were fourteen or so, he seems to bristle around me."

"It's your imagination, Coop." Yago stood and held out his hand to the Judge. "Thank you, sir, for your time."

Judge Covell extended his hand, rising behind his oversized desk. "I wish I could have been of better help. I'd be sorry to see a young man lose something so valuable to him." He led the two weary and disappointed men out of his office and to the front door.

Outside, they silently gathered their horse's reins and mounted up.

"I need a drink," Cooper said to Yago's back.

Yago turned in his saddle. "We need a good meal. I see an eatery up ahead."

"I can't think of food now," Cooper said. "I'll meet you at the saloon."

Yago made a grab for the bridle on Cooper's horse. "A meal first," he ordered sternly.

The tantalizing perfume of savory food met them the moment they stepped inside the Inn. They looked about and found an empty table in the corner of the room. The place was noisy with the clinking of tableware, the scraping of chairs, and the clamor of men talking.

"You could always marry Fanny," Yago offered reluctantly.

Cooper shot him a look that would stop the wind from blowing.

"Mother should have stopped pushing a long time ago, Coop. If she had, I think you'd have handled things just fine on your own."

Cooper toyed with the linen napkin in front of him. "Maybe, maybe not." And then he saw Rebel.

Chapter Fourteen

She was lovely. She was a brightly burning light, shining with confidence, radiant with belonging. Her glossy hair was loosely piled on top of her head, and her long, full skirt swished as she stepped toward them. A crisp white apron was tied at her slender waist, over an azure plaid skirt. She was a vision in blue and white.

She's blossomed here, he thought. *She's flourishing, self-assured . . . happy.*

"Well, sakes alive! What brings the two of you to Promise?" Rebecca said breathily. She gave Yago a winsome smile and ignored Cooper.

Yago answered plainly. "We came to see the Judge about a legal matter concerning Cooper. It's quite a surprise to see you here."

"Yes, I suppose it is."

Cooper couldn't tear his eyes from her. Her disregard pained him. *You never said goodbye. I'd have stopped you if I'd known. Why won't you meet my eyes?*

Rebecca threw him a glance, and he watched a blush crawl up her neck.

"Can you sit and chat awhile?" asked Yago.

"Mmmm, not yet," Rebecca said as she glanced

around at the busy Inn. "Never stop the plow to catch a mouse!" She'd tossed the words off lightly, but then was brisk and businesslike.

"I'll take your orders first and pour another round of coffee. Maybe then I can sit down and rest my feet."

"Bring me a big steak if you got one," Cooper said, trying hard to sound indifferent.

"Make that two," Yago seconded.

Rebecca nodded, disappeared through a door, returned carrying a coffeepot and strolled about the room filling cups. She moved with a smooth, fluid grace. Cooper's eyes were drawn helplessly to her trim waist, the way her tight bodice hugged her small, pointed breasts.

Suddenly Cooper realized his brother was speaking to him. "Wh-What?" It was an effort to pull his eyes back to Yago's.

"I said, why not ask *her*?"

Cooper knew what he meant. "No!"

"Now, just think on it for a minute," Yago hissed, leaning forward. "Mother would probably accept her better than she would a strumpet like Fanny. You already know Reb, so it wouldn't be like marrying a total stranger." Yago sat back in his chair and glared at Cooper, who was shaking his head. "Look, you can't have lived in the same house together for a year without becoming somewhat knowledgeable about each other! You know Rebecca is a good person. If we just explain the situation to her, she'll come around."

Entangled in his thoughts, Cooper wriggled in his seat.

"You could be right, except for the part about our mother accepting Rebecca." He felt claustrophobic in their corner of the café. "Maybe it could be a marriage of convenience, in name only," he said slowly.

Yago's eyes snapped up to a point beyond Cooper's shoulder. "She's coming."

Cooper drew a nervous breath and tapped his fingers on the table.

"Here you go." Rebecca placed their food before them and stood brushing off her hands.

Cooper began to dig into his steak with such fervor that Yago raised his eyebrows. "I thought you said you weren't hungry!"

"Starved," Cooper muffled through a full mouth. He looked up at Rebecca and swallowed. "It's good. Made just right." She smiled at him easily and left them for a table where a young man waited alone. She sat there with the customer, her back toward them.

"Looks like you have competition," Yago said.

Cooper studied the gangly young cowboy and shrugged his shoulders. "Don't look like much to me."

"You better hope he ain't much. She's been here a long time, and you two weren't exactly the best of buddies."

"We were better buddies than you ever knew."

"Really?" Yago raised his eyebrows again.

Cooper slowly cut his steak and looked up. Smiling. "Really."

Rebecca approached their table again.

"Judging by the way you're devouring that food, I'd say it's everything you wanted."

"Not quite," Cooper said. "We wanted your company, too."

"All right, you got it." She pulled out one of the extra chairs between them and sat.

"How's Daisy, and Chester and Blackie? And your family, of course?"

"Everyone is fine," Cooper said as his gaze traveled over her sweet oval face. "They miss you terribly."

"I could mention one person who doesn't." Finally she looked at him directly, with eyes that flashed liquid green fire.

"My mother."

"Is Madam all right?"

"We're taking good care of your cow, never fear," Cooper said.

"I'm sorry you weren't able to attend my wedding, Reb." Yago interjected. "Millicent and I had quite a shindig."

"I'm sorry too," she said with sincerity. Then she raised her chin, all business. "I owe you a horse! I've kept Buster at the livery here in town."

"Ahh, Rebecca, the horse is yours, you know that," Cooper said. He glanced at Yago as he wondered how to raise the subject of marriage. He ran his hand over the stubble on his chin. "Do you know the reason I came back home from Yankton?"

"Yes, I think so. It had to do with your father's death."

Cooper cleared his throat, shifted in his seat, and picked at a small piece of lint on the table.

"That's true. My father's will demands that I marry in order to inherit my share of the property."

He wanted to tell her he didn't give a damn about the money, it was just that his family needed him. Instead he cleared his throat again.

"There was a date by which I needed to get this accomplished. That date is fast approaching and, as you can see," he held up his ring finger, "I'm not married yet." He looked deeply into Rebecca's sea-green eyes.

She pursed her moist pink lips and threw a quick glance at Yago, who seemed to be sitting on the edge of his seat. She fingered the jeweled brooch pinned at her neck.

"Is this some sort of marriage proposal?"

Cooper relaxed, sprawling in his chair. He gave Yago a bold smile.

"Yes, ma'am."

"I think you'd better start from the beginning and

tell me the whole thing," Rebecca hedged.

Cooper felt his smile fade away. He took out the legal document and handed it to Rebecca, pointing to the proviso. She read it through slowly. He watched her thick, dark lashes flutter and one brow arch. She lifted her head and fixed him with a clear-eyed gaze.

"You could have had your pick. So why didn't you just marry someone?" Rebecca asked. "Jezreel or Carmella or—"

Cooper cut in, surprised at her attitude.

"You don't just up and marry somebody. You have to have feelings for them first. Why does everyone think I could just walk into a forced marriage?"

"I understand, believe me. When my parents died, the ladies of the town tried to induce me into marrying a dreadful old man. Remember stuffy old Mr. Aarsen? There I was barely eighteen and he was older than my father. So I understand. Nothing can make a person more obstinate. And yet, here you are, thinking of 'up and marrying' me, someone you have no feelings for."

Her smile seemed forced to Cooper, and her eyes seemed to be searching his for something he couldn't admit, even to himself.

Rebecca continued. "The will doesn't say how long the marriage must last, does it?"

"No. So?" questioned Cooper.

"Get a temporary marriage. Plan it with a divorce in mind."

The two men looked at each other.

"She's got it, Cooper!" Yago said.

"I don't know," put in Cooper cautiously, "it seems too easy, too simple an idea not to have been seen by the Judge or by David Dunn."

Rebecca raised her chin in acknowledgment.

"Let's talk to the Judge again. He's a good friend of mine." Her demeanor softened. "I know what it's like to lose your land, Cooper. I didn't have a choice like you might have."

Cooper felt the strain leaving his face.

"We'll all go and talk to the Judge, if you're able to get away, that is."

"I'll tell Tillie where I'm going." She turned to walk away and Cooper caught her hand.

"Rebel, thank you."

She smiled at him, face alight.

* * *

Judge Covell examined the legal document with more care. He took off his wire-rimmed glasses and looked at the small group gathered around him. "Becky is right." He rubbed his thumb along his long, sleek nose. "A temporary marriage could get you out of this situation without breaking anything in this will. You can divorce later."

Yago and Cooper stood and slapped each other on the back, grinning broadly.

"Well, boy, who you going to get to agree to a short marriage?" the Judge asked. "You got anyone in mind?"

"Me," Rebecca said.

Cooper's heart did a flip and beat hard in his chest.

The Judge swung around and looked at her in surprise. "Why in God's name do you want to do this? Is it because of Virgil? Becky, why this sacrifice?"

"It's not really a sacrifice, is it? After all, it will only be for a short time."

"Think of your reputation, my dear!" the Judge said. "Decent women in these parts don't divorce."

"What if something happens and things go awry?" Yago asked.

Rebecca shrugged. "What could go wrong? All that's required is that Cooper comes back to the Judge later to sign a divorce paper. No one else needs to know of the marriage except David Dunn."

"I don't think David will keep this secret," Cooper said. "He dislikes me too much."

"I'll handle David," Rebecca said firmly.

Cooper laughed at her apparent sense of power. "You, Rebel? I didn't know you two were acquainted. What makes you think he'll listen to you?"

"I have plenty to say to him. I am not going to share it with you, though, Cooper Conrad, so you can just wipe that curious look off your face. Just know he'll do as I say, I'm sure of it," she said.

"Rebel, Rebecca, you amaze me," Cooper said, shaking his head.

"Well, if all is settled, when do you want the beginning of this short marriage to take place?" The Judge stood, carrying himself with military bearing. With flawless timing, his wife appeared in the doorway.

"Maybe we ought to take a few days to discuss it further and think about it," Cooper said, guarding the last vestiges of his freedom jealously.

Rebecca would have none of his procrastination.

"We'll do it right now," she said.

"Now?" Cooper rounded on her.

"Sure. We have our witnesses here," She pointed to the Judge's wife and to Yago. "The Judge can marry us. The sooner you get a marriage certificate, the better it will go for you."

Yago chuckled. "

I'd pay good money just to see that look on your face again, Coop. She's right and you know it."

"Becky, are you certain of this?" asked the gray-haired woman, placing her hand on Rebecca's arm as if to hold her back.

"I'm just returning a favor, Angela. He helped me when I needed it the most, and now I'm repaying him."

"It wasn't me, Rebecca," Cooper said, feeling

abashed. "The credit goes to Malachi."

"Yago and Micah helped me, yes, but I know who held the ultimate decision-making power that day in Yankton, and it was you. All you had to do was put your foot down and I'd have been left behind. I know that." She looked Cooper squarely in the eye as if daring him to say otherwise.

Judge and Mrs. Covell watched the interplay between the couple intently. Angela caught her husband's eye and raised her eyebrows.

Yago cleared his throat.

"Well, let's get on with it, then."

The Judge took his cue, found the materials he needed, and asked the couple to join hands. Within minutes they'd signed a legal paper that claimed them to be man and wife.

"Rebecca to the rescue *again*," Cooper said wryly. Immediately he was sorry he'd spoken. He hadn't intended to sound snide.

"Reb saved Coop's sorry hide from a sidewinder once," Yago explained. He stepped forward and gave Rebecca a brotherly kiss. "Welcome to the family, Dakota Reb."

"Someday, Becky, you must explain that nickname to me," Angela said, smiling.

"I believe a toast is called for," the Judge said. "Angela, sweetheart, can you get us something to drink?"

Angela bowed her head and left to do as he'd asked. The Judge watched her go with love shining in his eyes, and then turned his attention to Cooper. "I'll draw up a divorce decree, whenever you feel enough time has passed to assure you of your property."

Cooper and Yago shook the Judge's hand. Angela returned with a tray of apéritifs in delicate long-stemmed glasses.

"How pretty and fragile," Rebecca said, holding her

drink to the light.

The Judge raised his glass. "To the duping of two fools: a loving father and a lawyer. And to the shortest marriage I've ever had the privilege to begin."

Rebecca kissed the Judge's silver-bearded cheek and Angela's soft one in turn. "Thank you," she told them both as she turned to leave. Cooper placed his hand protectively against the small of her back as he followed her down the steps. Yago trailed close behind.

* * *

Rebecca was very aware of Cooper's hand on her back and the warm tingles it sent up and down her spine. She marveled that he might keep it there for the duration of their walk, the entire length of the street. Her brain censured her, though. *Don't go making a first-class fool of yourself, Rebecca Marie.*

At Tillie's Inn, Cooper took her hand in his and gently turned her toward him. He towered over her by more than a head. When their eyes locked, he lavished his heart-stopping smile upon her and she thought she might melt.

"Ahh, Rebecca, you're unlike any woman I've ever known. What can I say?"

Yago looked away.

"Don't say anything, just kiss her."

Rebecca took a step back, pride and passion battling inside her. She held her head high.

"It's nothing, really. We'll just go on as if nothing has happened. It's just a favor, isn't it?" *Is that all it is to you, Cooper?*

"Rebecca! I can't believe a feisty girl like you would be afraid of a little thank-you kiss," Cooper said.

"I'm not afraid of kisses. I've been—" She stopped, her face flushing hot.

"If the sky weren't turning such a yellow shade of

gray, I'd like to hear more on that myself," Yago said, "but we better get a move on, big brother, before bad weather gets here."

Rebecca turned away, feeling a lump like a large squeezing fist in her middle. She was going to be living a lie. Her parents' union had been true and real. Now their only child had a sham of a marriage.

Chapter Fifteen

A sham marriage, Rebecca reminded herself for the hundredth time. Cooper would never give up his womanizing ways, married or not. The hateful thought stabbed into her brain. She slipped into her silky chemise and dimmed the lamp. The hour was late, and she knew she'd never get to sleep unless she faced the truth. She'd followed her heart again, like some helpless female, while for Cooper it was just a business arrangement.

She plaited her hair into a loose night braid and crawled under the bedcovers. *Plink!* She heard a noise at the window, and then another. *Clunk!*

She threw back the covers and tiptoed to the curtains, peering out cautiously. Below, swaying unsteadily, Cooper stood staring upward. Moonlight glinted on the whiskey bottle he cradled in one arm. He tossed another pebble. "Reb! C'mon, Reb, it's me."

He's here! Rebecca's heart leaped, then dropped. *He's drunk. He's beastly drunk and he's going to wake all of Promise with that noise.*

She opened the window and hissed, "Quiet! What are you—"

"Missush Conrad," Cooper called, "How many times

d'ye think you can run 'way from me?"

He lurched for the stairs.

"Coming up," he mumbled.

"No!" Rebecca cried, but Cooper had already begun to weave his way up the steps.

At the top of the stairs, he pounded on the outer door insistently.

"Rebecca Marie LaRoche Conrad. Lemme in, woman."

She persuaded herself it was just to keep him quiet that she hurried from her room to the outside door and unlocked it. He tottered into the hall and opened the first door he came to, the door to her bedroom. He wavered there, glassy-eyed, wearing a silly smile.

"I thought you and Yago were going home today," she whispered.

"He'zzat th' hotel. I persh—pershwayded him to stay." Cooper wobbled into the room and dropped heavily onto the bed, his long legs dangling over the side. "Dang it all, Reb! We never got a nuh—nuptial journey. A husband has rights." He raised his head and looked at her with glazed eyes. "I wanna kish—*kiss* those bootiful berry-colored lips."

He beamed his devilish smile, the one that made her heart turn over.

"You're inebriated. You must go."

"Sorry. I'm slightly sotted, it's true . . . ." He made a half-hearted attempt to rise and then collapsed again. "Y'know, I gotta confess, I wanted to sh—seduce you way back when . . . an' then when you dish—disappeared from the ranch, I searched f'you . . . couldn't find you . . . ." His words became incoherent and then dwindled away.

"Cooper, you can't stay here," she said, but he couldn't hear her. He began to snore gently.

Rebecca sat in the rocker and allowed her eyes a slow, delicious traverse of the length of him. The thick, dark hair she itched to touch, his well-cut mouth, lips parted slightly, his chiseled jawline, muscular torso, strong thighs. An old expression came to her: *Marry a handsome man and you marry trouble.*

She rose, tugged his boots off, and pulled her quilt out from under him. She wrapped it around herself, put out the lamp, and returned to her chair.

* * *

Rebecca awoke with a start, disoriented for an instant in the dimness. A rustling, stirring sound had roused her. "Wha—?"

"Hush—it's all right, Rebecca." Cooper loomed tall before her, shadowy in the subdued light. "Go back to sleep. It's not dawn yet." His voice became husky. "I'm so sorry I burdened you last night. I'll be on my way now."

"No!" She spilled the word without thinking.

He pulled her up to him, and the quilt fell away. She swayed there, her heart slamming against her chest. He cupped her bottom through the virginal white chemise and pulled her tightly against him.

She wrapped her arms around him, pressing even closer to his warm, muscular chest, feeling the strong beats of his heart. His mouth covered hers in an eager, hungry kiss that made Rebecca want to sink into it. His lips, hot and moist, tasted salty and delicious.

Cooper deepened the kiss into a leisurely, unhurried experience, melting her with pure pleasure. Then his mouth became less gentle—it seemed to consume her, devour her.

She whimpered hungrily, responding to his need and to her own. Her middle vibrated with want.

He broke the kiss like a drowning man breaking the water's surface. *Don't stop*, Rebecca moaned inside. She struggled to regain reason. Cooper had drawn away and held her out, away from him. In the predawn light she saw that his dark eyes were filled with concern.

"You've never *been* with a man before, have you?" he said gently. "You're chaste."

All she could do was nod. Suddenly she felt very mindful of her own slender body clothed only in a small, thin nightdress. A perverse thought stabbed into her consciousness, of the many attractive women who'd given themselves to Cooper. Rebecca knew herself to be decidedly lacking in voluptuousness. She must look mighty meager to him, she thought, deeply aware of her own inadequacies. Surely the hollows of her collarbones were visible in the half-light. Her breasts, high and firm, swelled the delicate fabric of her chemise, but they weren't the ample, luxurious kind. Stricken, she lowered her eyes.

He bent and touched his lips to the top of her head.

"You really don't have an inkling of how lovely you are, do you?" Cooper asked, his voice thick with desire. She felt his breath tingling her scalp. "You don't know how you affect a man's sensibilities. It was always so hard," he swallowed, "to be near you, your walk, your laugh, the clean scent of your hair."

Rebecca's heart flew in dizzying loops, and she knew. She knew beyond all concern that she needed and wanted this man, more than she'd ever desired anything. She looked into his eyes and lifted her arms to touch his soft, wavy hair.

"It's all right," she told him. "I want this. But with your experience and my lack of it, I'm afraid you'll think me clumsy or stupid or—"

He groaned and pulled her so close her breathing seemed to stop. In his sheltering arms she felt treasured, cherished. She ran her hands along the hair on his hard, strong forearms. He released her just long enough to slip his shirt over his head and he nestled her close again, tucking the top of her head under his chin.

She burrowed in, inhaling his masculine aroma, and felt his warm bare flesh against her cheek. She felt his deft hands moving over her tenderly, cleverly. She responded with every nerve ending of her burning skin. He lifted her easily, smoothly, off the floor, onto the bed, and kissed her hard. Rebecca's pulse raced. Her insides swirled with anticipation and delight.

When she gasped for air, Cooper took her face in his hands and asked, "Are you sure?"

She trembled so much inside she could barely whisper, "Yes."

He removed the last of his clothes then. "Your first time." He spoke throatily. "I'll make it good for you, I promise, my Rebecca."

My Rebecca!

His words filled her with elation. He lay beside her. She shivered at the touch of his hip and his long hard leg against hers. He rolled her on top of him; she felt his flat belly and his readiness, too. Everything in her pulsed and raced to that point, making her inhale sharply with exquisite pleasure. The thrilling surge of it spiraled through her. Her breath quickened.

The feeling was so new, so overpowering that she laughed out loud with joy. Excitement and curiosity made her bold. She slid a hand between the two of them and stroked the tight, smooth, hot skin of his hardness. Her feather touch elicited from him a rapturous growl of happiness. She marveled at the unfamiliar, unexplored territory of his body.

He grazed his lips along her neck, then cradled her head, guiding her mouth to his. Mouths fused, they moved together rhythmically and rolled over, clinging to each other as if to a capsizing boat. His hand cupped her breast, and with his thumb he stroked her nipple through the embroidered fabric of her chemise. Rebecca caught a quick breath as an electric current ran through her.

"Let me pleasure you," he breathed. He lifted the hem of her gown and Rebecca raised her hands over her head. He removed the garment with care, almost with reverence.

She gazed up at him unafraid, surprised at herself. She'd expected to feel embarrassment, but this was natural.

It was right.

Cooper bent his head and circled one of her nipples with his tongue. When he covered it with his mouth and suckled, a shiver of pleasure rippled through her. She threw her head back and dug her fingers into his buttocks.

He caressed the velvety soft skin inside her thighs, and slowly raised his hand to her mound. He lightly petted the soft, curly hair there, before his hand strayed to her belly. He made soft circular motions on her stomach, which seemed to vibrate under his palm.

She groaned, hungering for more. An exquisite ache in her center was building, building. Everything in her wanted to plead with him, beg him to take her over the edge, to drive himself into her.

He entered her slowly and began to move in short thrusts, rhythmically, and then more urgently, until they were plunging together, grasping at each other. Rebecca's body went taut, she clutched at him and uttered an ecstatic moaning sound she'd never made before. Rapture flared and flamed throughout her.

Perfection.

Cooper collapsed beside her, sated. She nestled into his encircling arms. For a time the only sound was their elated breathing.

"Is it always that wonderful?" Rebecca finally asked indolently, her voice dreamy.

Cooper laughed. "I believe it is. When it's done with someone you really care about, it is."

Do you really care for me, Cooper? she longed to ask. "Was it amazing for you, too?"

He nodded and smiled broadly, wickedly. A satisfied smile. Then his face softened and he said, "I was your first. Thank you for that."

"I should be thanking *you*," Rebecca said drowsily. "You do it so well." Warm golden light slanted through the east window now . . . soon Tillie would rise and would need her in the kitchen.

"You could come back with me, Rebecca." His eyes, the deepest possible shade of brown, slid away from her.

Reason fought with pride in her mind. *Why can't I tell him what he means to me? What am I afraid of?* She tried to keep her tone light when she said, "There's more to marriage than four bare legs in a bed, Cooper. Your mother and I can't live under the same roof. Besides, Tillie depends on me."

A darkling look had flickered over his face and was instantly replaced by a cool vigilance. He sat up and began to dress. "Who is Virgil?" he asked warily.

"Wha—?"

"Yesterday the Judge asked if you were going through with the ceremony because of Virgil." With his back to her, he sounded reserved, withdrawn.

"He's a friend, but . . . just a friend." *Who is halfway around the world and married, you dolt!* But something prevented her from explaining everything to Cooper.

* * *

Yago's horse pranced in place, eager to be off. Cooper doffed his hat to Rebecca and mounted up. "I'll let you know if David objects to this piece of paper. But you'd better be ready to travel, because he may want more proof."

"I'll come if summoned." She watched as their

horses trotted away. Cooper stopped at the end of the clay street and looked back. She waved. Cooper lifted his hat to her, and kicked his horse into a gallop to catch up to a fast-disappearing Yago.

She would never forget the sight of his leaving her.

* * *

The parched summer days crawled by in a haze of heat. To Rebecca it seemed as if the whole world had disappeared except for Promise. Very little outside news trickled in except for the report that Custer had lost his scalp in Montana Territory. The entire earth held its breath, waiting for fall to be ushered in, to be followed by a subdued, inert winter.

One evening when a band of Tillie's regular customers had gathered at the Inn, a spirited party developed spontaneously. Patrick O'Lear, a red-headed young cowpoke, drank too much and flirted shamelessly with Rebecca. Fair-skinned and sweet, at twenty-two he was almost Rebecca's age. She pinched his cheeks and humored him, remembering fondly how he'd come to her aid weeks before when a group of rowdy drifters had come into the Inn and pestered her.

Angela Covell added several dirty cups to the tray balanced on Rebecca's hip. Her knowing look echoed her words: "It seems Patrick has taken a real shine to you, Becky."

"Yes, I've noticed. The feeling isn't mutual, though I do like him very much."

"You're married to someone else, dear. It isn't fair to lead Patrick on."

"I'm *not* leading him on." Rebecca said. "Besides, my 'marriage' is spurious. It's a fraud. Cooper's just doing his duty to his family. His brothers need him there at the ranch, and—" Rebecca lowered her voice,

"Anyway, one woman would never be enough for Cooper Conrad." She sighed heavily, then felt a twinge as she remembered their early-morning lovemaking.

"If anyone could hold his attention, it would be you, my dear," Angela said. "The way he cottons up to you, anyone can see it plain as day!"

Gratitude and hope welled up in Rebecca at her words, until reality intruded.

"No. A cow in the field is a good thing, but if she gets into the garden. . . . Our union will be over as soon as the lawyer accepts it and we sign the divorce decree."

"What makes you so sure the lawyer *will* accept it?"

"He will, because I know something about him that he thinks no one knows."

"You'd blackmail him?" Angela asked, arching an eyebrow.

"If I have to, yes. It's for his own good, anyway. He's carrying around a grudge that can't be good for him or anyone else. Maybe I can get him to see that."

Angela looked at Rebecca in surprise.

"Cooper has a point in calling you 'Rebel'. You don't seem like the girl I thought I knew."

"You know me, Angela. This thing about David Dunn involves people I love and respect. Someday I may be free to tell you more, but right now I can't."

She shifted the tray on her hip.

"All right," Angela agreed slowly. "What about Patrick? He certainly keeps his eye on you."

They looked across the room to see Patrick studying Rebecca as he stood within a group of conversing men.

"I doubt he's heard a thing they're saying," Angela remarked.

Rebecca gave Patrick an indulgent smile. Angela cleared her throat and threw Rebecca a cautionary look before she walked away in search of the Judge.

Chapter Sixteen

Cooper looked at the poker cards in his hand, impatient for the last player to decide what to do. He raised a shot glass of whiskey, but it reached just halfway to his lips when he heard the call, "The stagecoach is in!"

"Rebel," he breathed. He finished the drink and stood, laying his cards down. "Sorry, fellas, I gotta go."

A smile on his lips, he strode away briskly. Behind him he heard one of the players ask, "What did he say?"

"He said he had to go."

"No, before that. He said 'Rebel'. Is that some kind of code?"

Outside the Gaspar saloon, Cooper took long, buoyant steps to the waiting coach and opened the door. Looking courtly and self-possessed, Judge Covell clambered out of the rig first, then took Cooper's hand and shook it vigorously.

Cooper turned and helped Rebecca from the coach next. His heart pumped hard as he kissed her soft, glowing cheek. His hand went to her slender waist in a proprietary manner. Then he escorted the pair down the street to David Dunn's place of business.

* * *

"What took you so long?" asked Cooper.

"A downpour between here and Promise," Rebecca said, her pulse skittering at his nearness. "You should have seen those poor horses, slipping and stumbling in the mud. I was sure one of them would break a leg and would have to be shot."

They stepped into David Dunn's office.

"The coach finally made it to the next post night before last. We had to stay put until the rain stopped and the way dried up some. The closer we got to Gaspar the better time we made."

"I'm glad to see you're all right," Cooper said, looking into Rebecca's eyes sincerely. Rebecca saw nothing but him, though the Judge stood by, erect and smiling.

"So this is Mrs. Cooper Conrad," David said.

Rebecca nodded, gazing at David's reserved, good-looking face. She was reminded of the daguerreotype of Luke. "David, this is Judge Covell," she said. "He performed the marriage ceremony."

"I know the Judge. Good to see you again, sir." A chilly look returned to David's eyes as he glanced back at Rebecca. "Tell me, Reb—" he pointedly stopped to read the name correctly from the certificate, "Rebecca, why is it you don't live with Cooper on the ranch?"

"My mother-in-law is opinionated and dictatorial. She's a bombastic, grandiose woman. I refuse to live there while she's in residence, and I would never push her out of her own home."

"I don't quite see Mrs. Conrad in that light. My own wife tells me what a dear Cooper's mother is."

"Your wife hasn't lived under the same roof with the woman. I have. Let me assure you, one year was quite enough."

David sniggered and looked at Cooper.

"Are you going to stand there and let her belittle your own mother like that?"

Cooper shrugged. "It's the truth."

David seemed at a loss for words; then he rallied. "Your marriage came awfully close to the closing date."

"Carrying on a courtship under the nose of my mother, who, I might add, was against it from the start, wasn't easy to do."

"How does she accept the marriage now?"

Rebecca blurted out, "She doesn't know about it, yet."

David's eyebrows rose.

"Really."

"You won't tell her, either. *Will* you, David?" Rebecca asked with threat in her voice as she stared him down across the pine desk.

"I was paid to look after Martina's interests and those of her children who already inherited."

"You mean you were paid to look after the interests of *all* the beneficiaries," Rebecca said, her ire visible to everyone. She turned to the Judge and Cooper. "I would like to speak with David in private, please."

The Judge nodded and started for the door. Cooper stubbornly remained fixed in place.

"Please," she said. He reluctantly followed Judge Covell outside where Coop stood in front of the office window, glaring in. The Judge placed a hand on his shoulder as if to calm him.

"David, your real mama and I are very good friends. I don't think she'd like seeing you treat your own brother this way," Rebecca said.

"What do you know about my mother?" David ground his teeth and scowled at her.

"I know Tillie, in Promise, and I know that your father was Luke Conrad. I know that Martina Conrad's children are your half-brothers and -sister. What I *don't* know is why you single out Cooper to hate and not the rest."

He pushed his face into hers. "Because I'm the oldest, not him. I should be getting a big share of the estate."

"I believe your mother wrote and told you it was Martina's money that made that ranch, not Luke's."

"What's that got to say to anything."

"It says if Luke had married *your* mother, maybe there wouldn't have been any big inheritance. Your daddy wasn't rich on his own. The money was Martina's and it belongs to her children."

She sat on the corner of David's desk, watching him intently.

"No one knows but me. I respect Tillie too much to tell her secret or yours to the rest of the world."

David searched her face. The fight seemed to go out of him. He sagged into his chair.

"I suppose you're right. Tillie wrote me a letter explaining everything. It's just been hard to let go of the resentment, I guess."

"You have just as much, if not more, than Cooper does. Tillie has told me of the loving care you received from the Dunns. Your adoptive parents couldn't be more devoted." Rebecca's voice rang with candor. "You're married to a beautiful woman, the only child of a rich rancher. You have a promising career. You have no reason to be jealous of anything the Conrads have."

"You're right, Rebecca," David admitted. "I'm no rancher, nor do I need the money. Since I was fifteen, I've kept the secret and yet I wanted to be a part of Luke's life. But I would never hurt the Dunns or Tillie by spilling the facts about me, a—a *bastard*." He shook his head slowly. "I wouldn't pain Martina, either. Thanks for making me see the truth of things. Is Tillie doing all right?"

"Feisty as ever. I love working with her at the Inn."

"I'm glad you're there for her. What will she do when you come back here?"

"I guess I'll have to find her a good replacement." Rebecca looked down at her shoes. She wanted to tell him that, probably, she would always be with his mother. But she couldn't let Cooper down. She hedged, "Tell me, David, would Cooper be in danger of losing his land if I divorced him?"

David's handsome face showed surprise at the sudden question. He looked into her eyes for the truth. "Why would you want a divorce, and so soon?"

"Martina will never accept this marriage. She'll make everyone miserable."

David continued to look her in the eye. "He wouldn't lose the land," he said softly. "Luke didn't think it through enough."

"Neither did you."

David shrugged. "I noticed the omission, but something stopped me from pointing it out to him. Maybe I needed my own revenge on the old man for abandoning my mother."

"I don't blame you for that. Do you want to tell him the good news, or should I? It would sweeten things, coming from you."

"Send him in," David said somberly.

When Rebecca opened the door, Cooper gave her a severe, probing look. Before he could say anything, Rebecca motioned him and the Judge in.

"He wants to talk to you."

Cooper looked past her at David and entered.

"Well?"

"I just want you to know the land is yours, no matter what happens." David took a deep breath and ran a hand through his thick fair hair.

Cooper's head flew around toward Rebecca.

"Rebel, explain this," he demanded sternly.

"No, I won't. You, Cooper, are going to accept things as they are, and you can thank David for having an understanding heart."

The couple faced off in a visual war for several moments.

The Judge broke the tension between them.

"Becky, I think it's time we found ourselves something to eat. The stage heads back to Promise in less than an hour."

"Yes, of course," Rebecca said.

Cooper had turned his intense eyes upon a nervous David.

"Are you going to see us off and count your blessings," Rebecca asked, "or are you going to stand here glowering at the one who let you off the hook?"

David began to chuckle as Cooper threw a surprised look at his wife. At David's amiable response, Cooper slapped his hat against his leg and good-naturedly muttered, "Damn you, Rebel."

He followed her out the door with the Judge bringing up the rear, laughing. Judge Covell stopped at the door and looked back at David. "Thank you, Dunn. If you were my son, I'd be darned proud of you." With that, he closed the door quietly behind him.

"Reb, I expect you to tell me what went on in there," Cooper insisted. "You're my wife. You must confide in me."

Rebecca leaned close to Cooper and whispered, "Temporary wife."

They all ate beef stew in the saloon. Rebecca took note of the low-cut dresses worn by the working girls, women employed to give men attention and to solicit their money. Cooper had always liked such women, she thought, as she studied them.

Cooper noticed her interest and seemed about to tell her something, but instead he addressed the Judge. "I'm sorry about eating in here, but it's the only place in town that offers food."

"That's quite all right. We'll be on our way in a minute anyway." The Judge adjusted his spectacles and flipped open his pocket watch. "We'd better head out, Becky."

Her heart plummeted.

Ask me to stay, she willed Cooper to say. He only looked at her with dark, liquid eyes. *Tell him how you really feel,* she pleaded with herself

But she wouldn't throw herself at him. She was too stubborn, too afraid. She'd been a woman of her own devices who could handle rejection from others but if Cooper spurned her, she couldn't bear it.

Resigned, she stood when the Judge rose from his chair, and walked with him to the waiting stagecoach. She took a seat beside the Judge and looked out at Cooper, standing on the boardwalk with his hat in hand. Neither of them had broached the subject of divorce. With a lurch that propelled her forward and back again, the coach carried her away.

* * *

In September an unfortunate cold spell had everyone snapping at each other. Tillie's Inn was empty of all but a few willing to venture out into the raw, gusty winds.

"Angela, have a nice, hot cup of tea and tell me what's got you down," Rebecca invited as she sat at Angela's table.

"Becky, I'm concerned about Adam. He's been out on the circuit for two weeks now and I haven't heard a word from him."

"Is that unusual?"

"Yes, he always finds some way to let me know he's safe." Just then a cold draft blasted across the room from the open door. Rebecca looked up and her face broke out in a welcoming smile.

"No need to worry any longer." She pointed over Angela's shoulder at the Judge's dignified figure.

"Adam!" Angela cried as she rose and embraced him. She tilted her head back, eyeing him with alarm. "Adam, you have a wheezing chest." She held the back of her hand to his face. "And a fever. Let's get you home."

"It's just a nasty cold," he said, his voice raspy. He began to cough.

"We're going home immediately to put you to bed. Thank you for the tea, Becky." She ushered her husband out and they quickly made their way up the street. Rebecca smiled at the sight of the genteel, loving couple, and she sighed.

Early the next morning a distressed Angela rushed into the café kitchen, wringing her hands. "He's taken a turn for the worse. We need a doctor." Her voice trembled with anguish. "It's bad. It's very bad." Tears slid down her cheeks.

Tillie wrapped her arms around Angela and gave orders to Rebecca. "Run over to the livery and send a rider for the physician in Whitebull."

Rebecca hastened to her task, then ran to the Covell's. Moments later all three women were at the Judge's bedside, doing what they could. Later Rebecca stole away briefly to write to Cooper.

* * *

"Here's a letter for Cooper. You'll see he gets it, won't you, ma'am?"

Martina glared at the little man behind the counter as she held out her palm for the envelope. "Yes, of course."

She turned and went on her way. Farther down the street, she glanced behind her once and then opened the missive. She read it rapidly several times over, her black eyes perplexed. She pocketed the message and hurried to David and Jezreel's splendid house at the end of the next square.

Martina shoved the envelope at Jezreel Dunn the moment she opened the door. "Look what came for Cooper. What do you think it means?"

Jezreel moved aside to allow Martina entrance at the same time she read the letter. She closed the door and looked up.

"Has Cooper gone to see a Judge about the will?"

"I don't know. Even if he has, what has that to do with that girl? I didn't even know he was in touch with her."

"Maybe he hasn't been. Maybe she wants to get in touch with him."

"But where does this business about a judge fit in?" Martina's voice surged with frustration.

"I don't think you want Cooper to get involved with her, do you?" Jezreel asked pointedly. "What's happened with his inheritance? The date for his marriage has past, hasn't it?" She sounded smug, even triumphant.

"I've asked him about it and he says everything has been taken care of. He's very vague about it."

"David is the same way," Jezreel said, losing her self-assured tone. "All he'd tell me is that the situation had been resolved."

"*Dios mío.* What if Cooper has married some girl in secret?" Martina began pacing. "He was involved with that brazen harlot Fanny and now he never goes to see her anymore. Do you think she has anything to do with all this secretiveness?"

"It may be that Rebel has something to do with it, Martina."

Martina stopped in her pacing and gave the blonde a level look. "What are you suggesting?"

"I think Rebel was mixed up with that judge somehow. I don't think you should give Cooper the letter."

"I don't like holding this information from my son."

Jezreel rolled her eyes in impatience. "Would you rather he become seriously involved with the little schemer?"

"No, I don't. Perhaps you're right." Martina's pacing brought her to the window. "The wind is picking up again. I'd like to get home."

* * *

The following day Martina's conscience finally bested her, and she handed the letter to Cooper at the table. She watched him read it and saw anxiety darken his expression.

"When did this come?" he demanded.

"What have you got to do with Rebel?" Martina countered.

"When did this come?" he repeated, voice harsh.

"Yesterday. What—"

Cooper cut his mother off.

"Why didn't you get this to me right away?" He jumped up, supper untouched. He threw on his jacket and headed for the door. Martina followed, grabbing at his arm.

"What have you to do with Rebecca?"

He shrugged loose and walked out, leaving his mother behind to close the door. He broke into a run, loping across the yard toward the stables.

Chapter Seventeen

Cooper pulled his cantering horse to a stop outside the Judge's home, sprang from the saddle, and ran up the steps. As soon as he saw the black wreath on the door, he knew he was too late.

Rebecca answered his knock. Her shining eyes were rimmed with a delicate pink, betraying the fact that she'd been crying.

"Cooper! You came!" She widened the opening and he stepped into warmth and light.

"I didn't get the message until yesterday." He rubbed the stubble that shaded his chin.

"But I sent it five days ago."

"My dear mother kept it from me. Have I missed the funeral?"

"No. Many people are still coming to pay their last respects. The burial is tomorrow. Angela's taking it hard."

Cooper turned at the swishing sound of silk skirts. Swathed in mourning, the widow walked to him.

"Angela," he said, "I'm so very sorry about your husband."

"Cooper, I'm afraid he can't help you anymore," she said vaguely, gracious even in the depths of her sorrow. "I'm sorry."

"Don't be. Your husband was a good man."

Angela began to weep with despair, and Rebecca guided her to the stairs. Cooper quietly removed his coat and sat waiting, hat in hand.

A soft knock sounded on the door. Rebecca came down to answer it and to welcome the visitors, Tillie and the red-haired cowboy Cooper had seen before. Rebecca introduced them. The young man frowned at Cooper.

Upon hearing the Conrad name, Tillie brightened, looking Cooper up and down appreciatively. He returned her glances, seeing a vestige of the beauty she'd once been. Her face must have been lovely once, but it had been ravaged by time.

The Judge had been laid out in his coffin in the dim, cold parlor.

"Who is he to Becky?" Patrick whispered, loud enough for Cooper to hear. Tillie just shook her head, her hankie pressed to her mouth.

More gentle knocking came at the door and Rebecca went to answer it again. Others followed. Rebecca's decorum and thoughtfulness with the callers impressed Cooper. She carried herself with confidence and grace and presence.

When the hour became late, and the last visitors left, only the original group of four remained. "I'll stay here with Angela tonight," Rebecca told Cooper. "Tillie can show you to my room; you can sleep there."

He nodded and silently followed Tillie and Patrick back to the Inn.

"This is the way to Becky's room," Tillie said the moment they crossed the threshold. "I expect you're wore out from traveling." They went up the stairs, leaving Patrick alone in the kitchen, fuming.

"Tell me, Mr. Conrad, how did you know the Judge?" Tillie asked, puffing from the climb.

"I met him through Rebel."

"Rebel? Who's Rebel?"

"I guess you call her Becky. We knew each other from before Rebecca came here."

Tillie left him then. Cooper had the room to himself. Rebecca's quarters were spotless, orderly and feminine, just as he'd remembered them. Cooper fell asleep almost the moment his head touched the pillow. But before he did, he breathed in Rebecca's clean, womanly scent from the linens. He smiled, basking in memories of the last time he'd been in this bed.

The following morning everyone in Promise gathered in a subdued cluster around the grave site to bid farewell to a well-loved man. Angela had pulled herself together and seemed to be managing fairly well. Gray clouds blotted out the sun; a chill breeze stung the mourners.

Afterwards, Angela pulled Rebecca and Cooper aside when most of the people had gone. "You two need to spend some time alone," she whispered. "Make some plans."

"My concern right now is you, Angela. Are you going to be all right?" Rebecca's face and voice modeled her compassion for the gray-haired woman.

"I've decided to go back East. I have a sister in Boston who'll welcome me. She's a matron. I'll be comfortable staying with her."

"I'll miss you."

"I have to write to Virgil. He'll feel bad about not being here," Angela said with a far-away look in her eye. Rebecca patted her hand. Angela continued, "I'd like to tell him about your marriage. Do you mind?"

"No, *I* won't mind." Rebecca looked up at Cooper with a query in her eyes.

Whoever or wherever this Virgil is, Cooper thought, *I'd be glad to have him know Rebecca's married to me*!

"Shall we go for a walk?" Rebecca asked Cooper.

"Lead the way and I'll follow." They grabbed their coats and strolled into the nearby woods. Fallen leaves crunched under their boots; a cold wind whistled among the bare branches.

"What do we do now?" Rebecca asked. "Perhaps we could find someone else to work with us."

"It wouldn't be handled as easily or discreetly as the Judge would've done. Neither of us would want a big circus of a divorce." He avoided her eyes and she his.

"Do either of us want this marriage?" She'd blurted out the words, but held her chin at a proud height.

Cooper wanted to take the pins from her hair and watch it cascade into a burnished sheet of chestnut and rich brown. He wanted to crush her slim-hipped body to his and kiss her perfectly-shaped mouth. *'Do either of us want this marriage?'* He'd tried to deny it, he'd ignored it all he could, but now he couldn't fight it any longer.

He loved her.

He carefully tried to make his words sound casual, while his heart thundered in his chest. "I'll accept it if you do."

He thought he could read a number of emotions as they crossed her face. Doubt, hesitation, dismay, regret.

"Cooper, I don't know. What about you? Are you willing to continue like this?"

Earlier his stubborn pride had kept him from admitting that she was the only one for him, and now it stilled his tongue. He could only nod.

"I'd like to stay here," she said. "I don't like the idea of returning to your mother's house. Tillie still needs me. You don't."

Yes, I do need you! he wanted to shout, but instead he perversely lashed out with the very thing he knew—he *knew*—he shouldn't say. "Tillie needs you, or is it you who needs the red-head, Patrick?" Jealousy made him hiss the words resentfully.

Rebecca froze. The color drained from her face; her large eyes turned a dark shade of murky green.

Cooper couldn't stop himself. The rivalry he felt consumed him. "Since you're no longer unsullied, I suppose you've taken him into your bed too!"

Her pained face flashed into fiery outrage. Before she could put her scalding indignation into words, he turned and stalked away.

Cooper felt shamed and guilty, bewildered by his own behavior. He set out for home immediately.

* * *

Yago met him as he came up the road under the Conrad crossbar. "From the fit Mother was throwing, I gathered you went to see Reb. Why?"

"Rebel wrote to me, saying the Judge was very sick, asking me to come. I ended up attending a funeral instead of getting a divorce."

"Cooper. I'm sorry. I don't think any of us could have foreseen this. How did it happen?"

"Pneumonia, while he was out on the circuit. By the time he got back to Promise, he was so sick the doctor couldn't help."

"How's Reb handling this?"

Cooper stopped his horse and dismounted to face his brother. "She refused to come back with me. Does that answer your question?"

"What you gonna do, Cooper?"

"I'll give her some time. Right now she thinks I'm a lout, and maybe I am. But, little brother, she's my chance for real happiness. More than I know anything, I know that."

Yago stared at him calmly. "I really thought she cared for you, too. I just figured she was playing hard to get."

"Rebel is Rebel. She doesn't play petty games like other women. If I know anything about that wife of mine, it's that she values her independence."

"A little too much, I'm beginning to think."

"Damn it, Yago," Cooper beat his hat against his leg in frustration, "don't you think that's occurred to me? I can't just grab her by the hair and tie her down to make her stay where she doesn't want to be."

"I thought she liked it here! What's she got against being here anyway?"

"Mother."

Yago's strong figure seemed to slump. "I have to confess, Coop. I told Mother about your marriage. She'll just have to accept it. There's no other way."

"Rebel is looking for another way. She suggested finding someone else to grant her that divorce."

Cooper, head bowed, turned toward the ranch house.

The moment he stepped inside, Martina confronted him, demanding explanations.

"Cooper, how could you have done such a despicable thing as to go behind my back and marry that low-bred, common—"

"Stop! Rebel is anything but common," Cooper ground out between his teeth.

"Let me see the marriage certificate." Martina held her hand out for the document. "I won't believe it until I see it."

Cooper snorted, opened the family safe and withdrew the leather-bound document, which she grabbed swiftly from his hand.

Chalina glanced at her oldest brother with sympathetic eyes, but she didn't say a word to bring her mother's wrath down upon her. She probably felt it best to be forgotten on this ugly day, Cooper thought. They watched their mother read the document.

"Yago!" Martina wailed, gaping at her son.

Chalina's compassionate eyes snapped to Yago, then back to her mother as Martina spoke shrilly again.

"You witnessed this marriage? I now have three sons under that woman's spell? How could you?" Martina stamped her foot in annoyance.

"I thought it would be best for Cooper to marry a girl like Reb, rather than a tart from a pleasure palace."

Martina gasped audibly.

"Reb is a decent, innocent girl. Cooper and I agreed it would be better to strike up a deal with Reb than to lose his inheritance."

"A deal? I suppose you offered her money to become your wife." Martina rounded, with open mouth, on her eldest son.

"No! She offered, as a friend. It was her idea to have a brief paper marriage to save my inheritance."

"She wants the family money and that's all there is to it."

Cooper's mouth twisted. He spaced his words, speaking bitingly. "There is no money, Mother. Oh, we're comfortable, and Chalina's inheritance is intact. But everything else is tied up in the ranch, and Norm Kearn didn't help any."

Martina stared at him blankly, then seemed to snap back. "But a marriage in front of a judge, Cooper, not even a church wedding," she said, lip curled. She began to pace like a caged panther. Suddenly she stopped and clapped her hands together. "Cooper, do you really want this marriage?"

The question had taken him by surprise. "I do," he said.

"Does *she*?" Martina asked, her voice rising.

His chest felt heavy. "I don't think so," he said. "What are you getting at? I won't have us dragged through a public scandal."

Martina, her onyx eyes snapping, seemed nearly euphoric. "This marriage, how many people know of it?"

"The Judge's wife, and David Dunn, Yago, now you and Chalina," Cooper said in a leery tone.

"I haven't told Millicent," Yago volunteered.

"This is the first *I've* heard of it," Chalina chimed in,

"You say this is just a paper marriage? You haven't—"

"What's are you thinking, Mother?" He eyed her warily.

"The church won't recognize this marriage," she said, defiance crackling in her eyes. "I'm sure the priest will have it annulled easily enough. Especially if you tell him it was not consummated. No one ever need know of it."

There was silence. It seemed to Cooper as if the bottom had dropped from his heart and left a gaping hole. It felt cold. *Rebel still has a way out.*

Chalina placed her hand on Cooper's arm in a comforting gesture.

"Yes!" Martina exclaimed triumphantly. "I'll tell the girl of it myself."

Cooper's regret became rage and boiled over, seething and ice cold at the same time.

"*Enough*! No more of your schemes, Mother. No more!" He bit off each word savagely.

Martina shrank from him, resorted to her tactic of filling her eyes with tears, and stalked off.

* * *

Rebecca stood in the kitchen doorway, lost in reverie. At the moment their only customers were a mother and her well-mannered child. The young boy had stared solemnly at Rebecca with wide, dark eyes beneath a smooth cap of black hair. If Cooper had a boy-child, she mused, he'd look very much like that. Strange feelings coursed through her, maternal feelings of pure, selfless love. She melted inside at the thought of carrying his baby, of raising such a beautiful child.

We're still married, but for how long? She felt a heartache similar to that she'd carried with her when she had first come to Promise and to Tillie's. She had worked hard, made many friends, , discovered things. She'd blossomed, thrived. She'd learned to use her womanly influence. She'd invested her money, but not her love, with the venturesome Scotsman, Virgil. She'd become as close as a daughter to Tillie, who'd confided in her the truth about David Dunn's parentage.

She'd thought she'd get over Cooper somehow, but then he and Yago had come to the Inn and everything happened so fast. The fraudulent marriage. David Dunn's acceptance of it. Grief stabbed through her as she thought of her deep friendship with the Judge and Angela, the loving couple whose days together had been numbered.

The day of the funeral, she and Cooper had parted so badly. He'd said a terrible thing that had made her feel sick. *Did he really believe I'd give myself so easily?*

Her pulse raced and warmth rushed to her center as she relived their early morning ardor the day after their marriage. He'd awakened delicious feelings in her. He'd brought her to life, and made her a woman. He'd aroused a hunger in her that only he could feed.

She heard Tillie come up behind her. "Not much business today," Rebecca commented to her friend.

"Becky," Tillie said slowly, "that Cooper Conrad sure was a looker, just like his father." She gave Rebecca an appraising look.

It was as if she'd read her mind. Rebecca studied her friend's lean, wan face.

"I don't know how to tell you." Tillie cocked her head, curious.

"Cooper's my husband." Her eyes never left Tillie's.

"He asked me to marry him as a favor, so he could keep his land. The Judge was to give us a divorce but he died before it could be done. Please don't tell anyone about it," Rebecca pleaded.

"I knew there was something there," Tillie crowed, "I sensed it—anyone could see it if they weren't blind. His eyes had more sparkle when you were in the room. He's a good man, I can tell. How did his old battle-ax of a mother take that bit of news?"

Rebecca laughed. "I doubt if she knows about it yet. If she does find out, she'll hate it."

"Good! It's about time something went against her grain. You know she'll come at you, don't you? Martina isn't one to sit still for things," Tillie said. "You'd better be ready for her when she shows herself, child." She smiled at Rebecca fondly. "Do you love him?"

"I love him. I always have." Rebecca had finally said it out loud. She sighed.

"Then you must miss him terribly. Let's sit down to a cup of tea and talk about it."

Appreciation for Tillie's insight washed over Rebecca.

"It's funny, really," she said. "I think of him almost constantly. I suppose that comes with unrequited love."

"You don't think he loves you?" Tillie asked in surprise.

"He doesn't." Rebecca saw bewilderment on her friend's face. "He calls me Rebel. To him, I'm a rebellious troublemaker he'd rather have no part of."

"For your own sake, girl, hang on to your man! I speak from experience. I should have had more backbone when I gave Luke up to Martina without a fight. Live up to that nickname of yours when Martina comes calling. Don't let her separate another couple." Tillie lowered her darkly silvered head, then raised it again, looking haggard.

Rebecca went over and gave her a hug.

"What are you going to do about Patrick?" Tillie asked. "He's still smitten, you know."

"I don't want to hurt him, but I am fond of him as a friend. He's very dear. Tillie, there's something else I have to confess to you."

"What could you have done that would be so awful?"

Rebecca took a deep breath. "I used what you told me about your son. I held it over him. He knows I got the information from you. I'm sorry."

"Maybe it's for the best. Forces united will stand," she said without bitterness.

"I hope, Tillie, you can still trust me not to misuse what you've confided in me. I wouldn't do anything to hurt you, ever."

"I know you won't." Tillie enfolded Rebecca in her wiry arms.

* * *

An early snow had dressed the area in pristine white. The two women sat at the table in the toasty kitchen, peeling potatoes.

Tillie sighed. "The natives are in such an uproar that everyone is staying near their homes and safety."

Rebecca remembered the last time she'd seen Little Bull right before she'd left the area in sorrow and anger just as his people had.

"It tears my heart apart. Soldiers and civilians have whittled away at the tribes until few of their young men are left. There have been raids and cruelty on both sides."

She shuddered as if to sweep such thoughts out of her head. "I'm in need of a change! I have a hankering to get out and race across the fields!" Rebecca said.

"Rebel," Tillie laughed, the crow's feet deepening at the corners of her eyes. "Maybe that name does suit you after all. If you're so weary of routine, maybe we should have a get-together, with music and dancing," she said, catching Rebecca's restlessness.

"Yes, let's!"

"On second thought, Cooper would never forgive me for letting his wife enjoy such a diversion."

"Oh, pooh!" Rebecca spat out. "He's forgotten all about me. He hasn't breathed a word in my direction."

"You weren't very forthcoming in sending any his way, either."

"Why should I? *She'd* just keep it from him anyway."

"True," Tillie reluctantly agreed. "But if you don't act like a wife soon, it may be too late."

Rebecca raised her eyebrow and gave her peeled potato a toss into the pot, making water splash.

"I won't run after a man, Tillie. I *won't*!"

Chapter Eighteen

Snow squeaked under Martina's shoes as she marched toward the waiting sleigh. Her breath steamy in the frigid November air, she pulled on her heavy mittens. Chester obediently helped her into the sleigh and covered her legs with blankets. The old man's moustache was white with frost and his movements slow in the cold. He climbed up and slapped the lines over the horse's back. The freezing temperature made the runners squeal as they slid down the path.

"To the church in Gaspar," Martina said. "I must speak to the priest." Then she mumbled, "Something has got to be done about that boy's mooning. It was almost better when he made use of that Fanny creature." She pulled her scarf tighter around her head.

* * *

The church was shadowy and cold inside. Martina's footsteps resounded in the otherwise silent space. She stopped before the statue of the Madonna.

"Can I help you?" the elderly priest said quietly from behind her.

Martina turned. "I have come to you to get an

annulment of my son's marriage, *Padre*." She delved into the pocket inside her cape and pulled out the leather-bound document.

"As you can see, the wedding wasn't performed in the Church. And they live apart. She is in Promise and he lives at the family ranch near Moskee's post." Martina impatiently watched the priest's thin, wrinkled-parchment face as he looked over the paper.

He raised his head. "The two young people should come and see me and we will talk about it then."

Martina gestured dismissively. "That won't be necessary," she said, her voice hard. "The marriage was an impulsive mistake, a misunderstanding. It should never have taken place to begin with."

"Nevertheless, I need to speak to both of them. There may be other circumstances involved that I must know first."

"Like what?" she asked stridently. "I've already told you the circumstances."

The old priest shook his head stubbornly.

"I've been a parishioner here for years. I would never separate my son from his wife if it weren't for the best. Father Coleman would have understood."

"Father Coleman is no longer here. I am." He gave Martina a significant look. "Tell the young couple to see me and I will consider the annulment."

"Of all the—" Martina turned on her heel and hurried from the dark, quiet church.

"Take me home!" she hollered at Chester, who raised his eyebrows at the outburst. She climbed into the sleigh clumsily without waiting for his assistance. Chester flicked the long lines and the sleigh protested its way back home again.

* * *

Cooper had been staring off into space when Yago

strode into the study, whistling a tune.

"Let's go into town for supplies and a drink. My wife is definitely showing her pregnancy and it may be a long time before I'm free to have any kind of fun."

"Sure, why not."

Most of the early snow had melted, leaving scattered patches of white like ragged scraps of linen caught in the sagebrush. The horses were frisky and spoiling for a good run in the mild weather. Cooper and Yago let them have their way, heading toward Gaspar at a full gallop.

Together they reined in their horses before the general store. "To tell the truth, Coop, the only provision we have to pick up today is some chew for Blackie," Yago said. "Will you do that while I look for something for Milli?"

Inside, Cooper stepped up to the counter. "How you doing, Calvin? I need a pound or so of chewing tobacco." He watched as the small, thin man went to weigh out the chew.

"Say, I got a letter in the back that just came," Calvin said as he handed over the cloth bag of chew. "Haven't sent it on to the tradin' post yet." He disappeared into the rear room and came forward with an envelope. He handed it to Cooper and pointed at the writing on the front.

To: Becky LaRoche Conrad, in care of Moskee's Post, Wyoming Territory, United States of America

"Do you know her?"

"Yep. Happens to be my wife." Cooper looked at the return address and his brows shot up. "Scotland?"

"Yep. Never knew you was married," Calvin said. "I knew a man by the name of LaRoche back in my salad days." His eyes glazed with a far-away look, remembering.

"He married a pretty little gal, Marie. Her pa was in the cavalry stationed by Fort Yankton, if I remember right. LaRoche hisself was raised by Indians. He told me so . . . his mother was Sioux and his father was a trapper. He got one look at that little gal and decided to settle down to farming. Imagine that!

"He'd been a good teamster for the cavalry. He hauled a lot of my stuff. Good with a whip too. Handled it like it was part of hisself."

"Sounds like my wife's parents, all right," Cooper said, pleased to hear it.

"Don't know what happened to them," Calvin continued. "I lost touch when I moved on. I got a sister back there, though, and a niece. Didn't get on too well with Wright, my brother-in-law."

"I knew the Wrights when I was there," Cooper said. "Liza is your niece? I used to spark her, off and on."

"You don't say! Small world. I should have her up here for a visit sometime. My missus would like that, seeing we don't have any of our own." Calvin watched Yago come forward with a bright red ribbon in his hand. "A pretty for the little lady, hey?"

Yago colored. "Yeah, I guess so."

"Well, nothin' wrong with that. Should happen more often than it does," Calvin said as he wrapped the ribbon for Yago.

"Let's get that drink," Yago said to Cooper when he had his purchase in hand. "What's that?" he asked, pointing to Rebecca's letter.

"A letter for Rebel, all the way from Scotland. I'm real tempted to open it up and read it."

"Well, she *is* your wife . . . ." Yago shrugged his shoulders and followed Cooper to the saloon.

Seated at a corner table, Cooper could bear it no longer. He felt guilty doing it, but he rashly tore open Rebecca's letter and read silently:

Dear Becky,
Angus informs me our miners have hit the mother lode. They're calling it the Homestar Ledge. We increased that investment for you just as I said we would. Congratulations, darling, you are now a rich woman in your own right. Angela wrote me of your marriage. I hope you'll be very happy. You are still in a large part of my heart.

Love always,
Virgil

Cooper stared at the letter. "My God."

Yago leaned forward in his seat. "You gonna explain that?"

"There goes our mother's theory that Rebel married me for my money." He handed the paper over for Yago to read. It wasn't the money he was thinking about, but the unwanted pains of jealousy. His chest restricted as the words kept drumming through his mind: *You are still in a large part of my heart.*

Yago just whistled softly. "What you gonna do, Coop?"

"First thing, I'm laying down the law to Mother, and then I'm going to get my wife. She's had enough time to get used to the idea of me."

"You gonna show this to her?"

"Yup," Cooper said just before he raised the shot glass to his lips and threw whiskey down his throat.

* * *

Cooper went in search of Chester when they rode into the yard. He wanted a fresh mount readied for him after he'd set his mother straight about Rebel. The old cowhand was nowhere to be found. He poked his head into the mess house. "Blackie!"

The cook shifted his ponderous figure from the stove. "Yes, Coop, boy, what can I getcha?"

"Where's Chester?"

"The missus came for him this morning to take her to Moskee's. She told Chester that her and Chalina was tired of being cooped up and wanted to see some country, so they were going to catch the stage for Promise. Be back in five days."

"Like hell!" Cooper said as he slammed the door and sprinted for the stables. Within five minutes he bolted from the yard on the back of a big black gelding.

* * *

"Mama, why are we going to Promise? You aren't going to interfere in Cooper's affairs again, are you?" A sudden jolt forced Chalina to grab onto a strap to keep from being thrown to the floor of the stagecoach.

"Someone has to do something. You've seen how he has buried his head in the sand because of that uncultured, unsuitable girl."

Chalina rolled her eyes in distaste at her mother's words. "Maybe he's waiting for Reb to make some decision first. Your going to see her is a big mistake."

"If I want your opinion, young lady, I will ask for it. What do you know about the affairs between and a man and a woman, anyway?"

Chalina drew back into her seat and sighed with resentment. She'd learned a long time ago that, when her mother's dander got up, it didn't help a whit to argue with her. *I hope Reb stands up to her*, Chalina thought. She stayed uncharacteristically quiet all the way to Promise, her foot tapping angrily on the floor of the coach.

* * *

"That inn over there." Martina said, pointing. "I believe that is where Yago said she is employed." She gathered her skirts together, ready to alight from the stage.

Chalina put her hand on her mother's arm. "Please, Mama, leave Reb and Cooper alone."

Martina shook off Chalina's hand. "Nonsense! I only have their best interests in mind. Are you coming, *querida*?"

"No, Mama. I see a store over there with a pretty hat in the window. I think I'll stroll over that way instead."

"You'll know where to find me," her mother said as she marched forward.

Chalina gazed at her mother's straight back for a moment, drew in a deep breath and quietly said to herself, "I don't like this."

* * *

Rebecca stopped short in the kitchen doorway when she recognized the new customer. She turned back and uttered Tillie's name.

The thin older woman glanced out to see what was going on. "Oh, Lord!" She drew a great breath. "Just remember, Cooper calls you Rebel. I suggest you live up to it."

Rebecca squared her shoulders and stepped forward, a smile pasted onto her face.

"Mrs. Conrad, how nice to see you again." She glanced heavenward beseechingly. *Forgive me, Lord, for that white lie.*

Martina looked her up and down. "Well, I see you're looking presentable. I suppose Cooper has given you money for new clothes."

Rebecca couldn't stop herself from fibbing again.

"Yes, he's been a very good husband, supporting me well." She wondered if lightning would strike her dead for the falsehood.

"Of course he has. I've raised him to be kind to others." Martina's black eyes were glacial.

"Then you've done a very good job, Mrs. Conrad. He's one of the kindest men I've ever known."

"I'm going to be frank with you, Rebecca." Martina narrowed her eyes. "I've come to ask you to give my son an annulment. I've already spoken to our parish priest and he has told me it can be done swiftly and easily. All you and Cooper need to do is come and talk to him about it. I'm sure you could convince him that it would be for the best."

"Convince who? Cooper or the priest?"

"Why, the priest, of course. Cooper has no objections to an annulment."

"I think I'd rather have Cooper come and tell me this himself."

"He has no time for running after women who cling to him," Martina said.

"I would say it was the other way around, Mrs. Conrad. Cooper needed *my* help."

Martina shot her a challenging look. "How much money do you want, to get this marriage annulled?"

"I took no money to get into this marriage and I'll take no money to get out of it."

"That's my Rebel." The words were spoken proudly in a deep, rumbling voice.

Both women's heads swiveled toward the door. Cooper stood just inside, with his arms crossed in front of his chest. He unfolded them to stride toward the women, and when he reached them, he leaned over and kissed his wife's gaping mouth. After a long, breathless moment, he released her lips to look deeply into her eyes. He ran the back of his hand tenderly along the curve of her cheek. "I knew you couldn't be bought off."

The sight of him stunned Rebecca. His rangy, long-limbed body looked splendid in denim pants and a red flannel shirt that suited his dark coloring perfectly. His firm jaw, his piercing gaze, his rakish grin—all of it dazed her.

Martina broke the spell between the couple. "That's quite enough."

"Here, Rebel," Cooper said, handing over Rebecca's letter, "this came for you. I opened it—I'm sorry."

Rebecca read the letter and looked up to Cooper for his reaction.

"Angus informed me some time ago of their—our—financial success," she said calmly.

"Maybe you'll allow Mother to see the letter," he suggested. "It'll show her once and for all you're not interested in the Conrad money." He paused, then continued more softly. "We do have very different backgrounds, Rebel, but I know what a kind, loving, giving person you are. And my mother will learn to accept you."

Cooper turned to Martina.

"Rebel has the grit, strength, and wisdom to make me the best wife I could ever want."

Rebecca inhaled sharply, hardly believing what she'd heard.

Martina opened her mouth to speak, but closed it again when Cooper cut her off. "There will be no annulment!" He grabbed the letter out of Rebecca's inanimate fingers and slapped it down in front of his mother. "Read it!"

Martina looked up from the letter with one brow arched.

"I just wanted what I thought best for my son," she said bitterly.

"Mrs. Conrad, you've been sadly mistaken about me. I'm not a wicked woman," Rebecca said in a strong, commanding timbre. "It's true I can be headstrong and stubborn, just as you can be. But I believe I'm a good person. Are you?" Her gaze never wavered, but then her tone softened. "I do understand how much you must love your son."

I love him, too, Rebecca thought. His words, "the best wife I could ever want," seemed to echo in her head until she felt dizzy. She didn't want to be alone in life, like Tillie, broken-hearted. But Cooper had much to gain and nothing to lose from marriage to her, didn't he? If only she could be sure he truly loved her. Confused, almost groggy, she rubbed her temples as if to force some sense into her brain.

"Please go. I must think," Rebecca said, fighting for control over her emotions.

"Why, Rebel?" Cooper asked. "I know our marriage didn't come about in the normal way, but I think we would suit."

Rebecca felt as if she were drowning in his penetrating, pained eyes.

"Cooper!" Chalina shouted from the door and ran forward to give her brother a kiss on the cheek. "Is Reb coming home with us?"

Cooper's pleading eyes met Rebecca's and he waited for her to answer. After a long silence, Rebecca said, "Not now." She felt sick to the core and thought herself a fool, but she couldn't think straight at that moment.

Chalina rushed to Rebecca and hugged her. "Please, Coop loves you so. I know he does." Genuine compassion filled her heart-shaped face.

Martina thrust her chin upward, took Chalina's hand and pulled her toward the door. "We'd better go catch the stagecoach, *rosa.*"

Cooper turned to Rebecca and stubbornly set his jaw. "I'm not giving up on you. I'll be back to take you home where you belong." He backed out the door, never taking his anguished eyes from Rebecca's.

"How much do you want me, my darling?" Rebecca whispered to his receding figure.

* * *

Tillie entered her room later, carrying a stack of clean, folded laundry. "I tried hard not to listen down there," she said, "but it seemed to me that boy wants you, child! What are you going to do? Never mind, it isn't my business anyway." Tillie's pinched face turned red. "Sometimes I shoot my mouth off."

"Oh, Tillie, I don't know if Cooper wants this marriage because of me or my Homestar money. And I would die if he took a mistress. It would kill me." Rebecca hesitated, weighing her thoughts. "Besides, Martina is unbearable. Would you want me to give myself over to a situation that would be difficult and unhappy? I wish for Cooper to prove himself somehow."

"Rebecca, why? My stars, for the two of you, no one exists but each other. I'll allow you're up against it with that cussed mother of his, but you're just as strong-willed as she is, maybe more. If you love Cooper, why not keep him?"

Rebecca stared into space, mixed-up and miserable.

"Cooper said he was coming back for you. When do you think he'll show up?"

"I don't know, but it may be soon. Why?"

"I think scheduling our social for tonight was perfect timing." A smile brightened Tillie's pale features. "I'm hungry for some music and fun. How about you?"

Chapter Nineteen

Cooper eased himself in the door quietly; no one paid attention to one more soul joining the crowd of partygoers. The warmth and music and laughter inside contrasted greatly with the cold night air and with the chill he'd experienced here earlier in the day. He'd come this evening to get his estranged wife, but he'd walked into a rollicking spectacle.

It seemed all of Promise had turned out. Single men roamed between small clusters of eligible young ladies. The tables and chairs had been shoved to the perimeters of the dining room, leaving the center free for dancing. Several musically-inclined cowhands stood on a makeshift bandstand, playing their fiddles. Enamored couples sat at tables in the far corners, away from the well-lit center of the room. More lanterns had been hung over the tables laden with party fare. People were bumping into each other on the dance floor, voices shouting to be heard over the din.

That Rebel could be part of this clamorous behavior set Cooper's teeth on edge. No wonder she wouldn't come home. How often did she get involved with these goings-on? He searched for her in the crowd, his eyes roving over the room several times. Just when he thought she wasn't there, he saw her standing in a dark corner, and she was with a man.

He made his way slowly, but he kept Rebel in his sights. His anger flared with what he saw as he drew nearer to them. The lanky red-headed cowboy, Patrick, had his arm around her, pulling her close.

The young man seemed to be pleading his case to Rebecca. "Becky, I've known you for a long time now and I think I ought to have a kiss or two." Whiskey had made him sleepy-looking.

Rebecca placed her hand on his chest for leverage to keep him at a safer distance. "Patrick, please, this isn't right. I have something I should tell you, but not now. Tomorr—" Cooper seized her arm; she spun to see who it was.

"Rebel, pack your things. We're going," Cooper ordered gruffly.

Patrick swayed. "Now, wait just a minute. The girl is mine."

"Yours?" Cooper said. He looked at Rebecca significantly. "You didn't tell him?"

Rebecca simply stared, her luminous emerald eyes wide.

Patrick squinted from one to the other before he spoke. "Now, see here. We were havin' a right good time. Nothin' wrong with that. Who are you to Becky, anyway?"

Cooper gave Rebecca another meaningful look.

She continued to gaze at him, her cheeks coloring.

"I'm telling you, Rebel, I will drag you home if I have to. By God, I will." He realized he still held her arm, and dropped his hand. His breath came quick and shallow to keep up with his rapid heartbeat. Inside himself he cried out to her, *I need you. I can't let you go.*

Cooper enveloped her hand in his and began pulling her toward the kitchen door, toward the stairs to her room.

Patrick possessively grasped Rebecca's arm. "I don't think the lady wants your company."

Cooper's upper lip curled in warning as he turned back to Patrick. "My *wife* will have my company whether you agree or not."

Patrick threw his head back slightly as if dodging a fist. "Wife?" He said it as a whisper, barely heard. His attention centered on Rebecca now. "Becky?"

Rebecca wiped the moist palm of her free hand on her skirt. "I wanted to tell you, Patrick. I just never got the chance to explain."

Patrick looked whipped. He stared vacantly down at the tips of his boots. Then he nodded his head, turned, and walked away.

Cooper put his lips close to Rebecca's ear and whispered, "Let's go upstairs."

She gasped and responded to the gentle tug of his hand by following him like a lamb.

Cooper led her up the passageway, and she closed her bedroom door quietly behind them. Here the noises of the activities below were muted. She lit a lamp and turned the wick down low. Then she whirled to face him.

"How dare you tell them I am your wife!" She stood with arms akimbo, hands on hips, leaning forward slightly.

Cooper wasn't prepared for this turn of events. As if he were speaking to an obstinate child, he exaggerated every word.

"You *are* my wife!"

Rebecca took a deep breath, straightened her spine, and jutted out her chin in defiance. She began to pace back and forth, her hips swaying. The motion mesmerized Cooper—her tiny waistline, her undulating hips, her enticing body were like forbidden candies within a child's reach.

Rebecca must have read his thoughts, for she threw

a quick glance toward the bed.

Cooper saw it and chuckled. "Oh, yes, lady mine. Tonight I'm going to make you know you're my woman." He strode to her, caught her lightly around the shoulders and pulled her into his arms.

"My wife."

She pushed away, her rebellious eyes snapping.

"Where will I go now? After your announcement below stairs, I can't stay here. Everyone will know by this night's end that I'm a married woman living away from her husband. I'll be looked down upon, branded as a shamed woman. And I won't live like that again. Not *ever*!"

Cooper read fear and pleading in her defiant green orbs.

"No one will hurt you again. I won't let them." His arm snaked out and around her middle and slammed her forward against his chest. He felt her soft breasts against him, smelled her cinnamon and vanilla scent.

"Rebecca, you're a fascinating, capable woman who deserves respect. You're earthy and honest and real." He stroked her soft hair soothingly. "I know circumstances in the past have forced you to wear a hard, protective shell around your feelings. I've been hiding from my own heart, too. Pain can come from love. Just look at my parents' marriage."

She tilted her face up and Cooper saw yearning written there. Her lush mouth trembled.

"You're afraid of being tied to a shrew, aren't you? One who would plague you with her carping. That's something I could never be, don't you know that?"

"I finally understand. My arms have been so empty, my bed so cold without you!"

"So while I've been here mooning about you, you've been . . . ?"

"Hungering for you." His breath caught in his throat. Heat and need flared in him; his mouth descended onto hers with a bruising kiss. She tasted fresh, delicious.

A burst of laughter erupted from the people below, insinuating itself between the two of them. They lifted their heads. Cooper's heart raced.

"Say you love me, Cooper. Make me believe that you love me. I'd come home with you in a second if only you would truly love me."

Cooper looked into her incredible eyes and saw that they spoke eloquently of the truth. He marveled at the sensations that rocked him. He felt a sense of wonder with her that no other woman had given him. "I do love you." *I finally said it and it was right.*

His hands cupped her small, rounded bottom and pulled her up to his maleness. She was all there was, and she was his.

"You would choose me over Virgil and Patrick and anyone else?"

Her green gaze was bold and impish at the same time.

"Of course. I'm besotted with you." Then she raised her fine, arched brows and asked, "How about you, Cooper? You've always had females, lots of females."

"There have been other women in my life. But none like you. There never will be any other for me. You make me thirst for things I never thought I believed I wanted. A wife. A home of our own. Children."

She placed her hands on the hard curve of his biceps, shook them playfully and laughed.

"A reformed rake makes the best husband, they say."

"Any more of your witty remarks before I kiss you?" he said, and he took possession of her lips. She became soft and yielding against his hard body. He enfolded her to him tightly, tightly. Sharp heat knifed through him; his blood rushed and filled him and he was hard as a stone. His breathing became rough, labored.

Rebecca ripped herself away, her inhalations as ragged as his, and held his gaze as she began to undress. The long, slender column of her skirt slid to the floor in a silken puddle. Still holding his eyes captive, she teased him, running her fingers slowly around the low, square neckline of her bodice. The creamy skin of her décolletage drew him in.

She turned her back to him, and he began to undo the many tiny covered buttons. The tailored satin bodice molded to her, snug over her hips. Rebecca cast the bodice off, then led him to the bed. She sat on the edge and put her feet out to him for him to remove her dainty heeled boots.

He knelt before her and took one of them on his knee. He ran his hand over the soft kidskin, then worked the spherical glass buttons free. He gently tugged the footwear off and slowly, sensuously peeled her stockings off one by one.

Rebecca's chest heaved when Cooper sat close beside her on the bed. Conscious of the heat emanating from her, he began to unbind her corset. When it fell away, she stood and slipped out of her petticoat.

He stood, too, finding himself unsteady on his legs. He laughed, delighting in the lovely sight of her in the white, lacy chemise. "Quite a few more items of clothing than last time we were here together, hmmm?"

She grinned back at him, but he saw that she trembled. He helped her pull the chemise over her head, and her drawers to her feet so she could step out of them.

Together they fell onto the bed, he skimming his fingers over her silky skin, she straining, pressing herself into him. Cooper urgently needed more of her, but he wanted it to last forever. He forced himself to slow down, allowing his tension to build up to even greater heights. He buried his face in her breasts and breathed in her clean, womanly scent.

Rebecca slid her fingers behind his ears and through his hair; it made every nerve ending in his scalp come alive. He licked one of her nipples and lightly blew on it, making her shiver. He turned to the other breast and sucked greedily.

"Mmm, yes," she murmured thickly, arching into his hardness. With her fingernails, she lightly traced the contours of the muscles of his shoulders, his arms, down to his hips.

She was driving him mad with anticipation, and still she plucked more sensations from his pulsating body. She grabbed his hips and began to grind against him, swiveling her own hips and nearly taking him to the place of no return.

Cooper felt himself drowning in the passion, but he wouldn't let go. Not yet. He leaned on one elbow and looked into her extraordinary eyes. He ran his hand over her breasts, moving from one hard nipple to the other, then trailed his fingers down to her moist center. Gently, he pushed through the lips and folds there and found her tiny bud, caressing it with an exquisitely light touch.

She groaned, quivering, and rocked into him, seeking release. Cooper felt so weakened from need that tremors ran through him. Her body enveloped him and he joined with her, thrusting, falling into nirvana as the world sped away for both of them. His woman Rebecca, his love, cried out joyously and an eruption of ecstasy spread through his body too.

"Rebel. Oh, God!" Breathing heavily, they lay side by side, deliciously satisfied. Cooper gathered her closer, bringing her head onto his chest and her womanly softness against him. A flood of devotion washed over him as he thought, *We've just shared the deepest human intimacy possible. I never want to lose that with her.*

"Always remember, my love," Cooper spoke thoughtfully, wholeheartedly. "I didn't marry you for my inheritance. I knew even then I wanted you forever."

Beside him, Rebecca purred and stretched like a contented cat. "I guess you can't tell the depth of the well by the length of the pump handle," she said, eyes twinkling.

Cooper laughed as he idly rubbed a strand of her shimmering tresses between his fingers. "I like your hair better this way, unbound, all loose and lustrous. You do look mighty fetching, Miz Conrad."

She made a demurring sound and shot him a skeptical glance. "I detest the little bump on the bridge of my nose, you know. It's the one thing I wish my father hadn't given me."

"But it suits you perfectly," Cooper argued. "It fits in harmony with the rest of your beautiful face."

Rebecca rose, a dubious look still on her face, and put out the lamp. The party below had quieted; the room filled with peace and blue moonlight. Cooper gazed about, taking measure of Rebecca's possessions. "You don't travel as light as you used to," he chortled. "In the morning we'll pack up the horses."

Happily exhausted, they fell asleep as the noises downstairs dimmed.

* * *

The brilliant ball of sun perched on the black horizon, reddening nearby trees and buildings. Rebecca sat near the window, watching the blazing sphere ascend. She glanced over her shoulder and saw her handsome husband tinted by its red glow. She loved him so deeply it scared her, a little. She began to gather her belongings and pack them into cloth sacks that could be tied to the horses. She moved quietly but quickly; the task was done long before Cooper awoke.

In the kitchen, she talked with Tillie while they made breakfast. They spilled bittersweet tears and hugged each other copiously.

"What will I do now, child? I've grown used to having your help around here." Tillie wiped moisture from her eye with bony fingers.

"I've been thinking about that," Rebecca said, "and I believe the Johnson's girl would like to give it a try here. She'd be a good worker for you."

Both women turned their heads as Cooper joined them, looking rumpled and stubbly and adorable.

"My husband! I was just telling Tillie earlier of the tongue-lashing I expect I'll endure from Martina when we get back."

Cooper poured himself a cup of coffee and smiled.

"You can hold your own against her, my darling. You'll do just fine."

"Yes, I will." Rebecca took a deep breath and fixed him with her most direct gaze. "A long time ago, my mother advised me to keep resolve in my heart and to be true to myself. Cooper, it's not in me to change dresses three times a day and to order the help around. I won't alter who I am."

He chuckled and shook his head. "I wouldn't have you any other way, my Rebel." He grabbed a muffin and headed for the door. "I'm going to load the horses with your belongings, wife of mine."

* * *

Rebecca felt surprise at how easily she fit right back into the Conrad household and its routines. Cooper's siblings were more gregarious and receptive than ever. Her old friends at the ranch welcomed her back with open arms. At her emotional reunion with Madame, she found the yellow-brown cow fat, content and pregnant.

Rebecca's days were filled with buoyance and cheer in anticipation of nights spent in Cooper's arms. Now she regretted all the more those wasted months apart, when she could have been happily sharing his bed, his life. Even the undercurrent of opposition that flowed from Martina couldn't ruin Rebecca's ebullience, although, after visits from Jezreel Dunn, it was more pronounced than ever.

* * *

Rebecca peeked out the window of the upstairs sewing room when she heard the sound of an approaching buggy. She saw Jezreel Dunn alighting, and she wasn't alone. Another familiar blonde emerged from the buggy, and Rebecca felt apprehension flit through her. "Liza!" Her heartbeat accelerated with the realization that soon she would be expected to go down to the drawing room and make pleasant conversation with someone who knew her past, knew how others had tried to humiliate and shame her. Someone beautiful to whom Cooper had once been attracted.

She took a deep breath and squared her shoulders. There was nothing to be done but to face her past. First, however, she went to her room and quickly tidied herself in front of the looking glass. Her hair was up in a becoming style and her clothes were of the latest fashion. She had filled out; her body curved in the proper places. "Maybe Liza won't recognize me," Rebecca told her image. She tilted her chin up and went to face them.

Martina stood by, simpering, as Jezreel presented Liza to Chalina. The contrasts between the whiteness of the blondes and the darkness of the brunettes looked startling to Rebecca. She stood transfixed in the doorway a moment, until she heard Jezreel pronounce her name in introduction. "Rebecca, I believe you already know Liza."

"Yes, Liza, it's nice to see you again." Rebecca stepped lightly forward and held out her hand politely. Liza briefly touched it without removing her fine leather gloves.

"Rebel," Liza said, and her eyes sought Jezreel's. A conspiratorial look passed between them.

Rebecca felt her face grow warm and her dander rise.

"You know each other?" asked Chalina, her brown eyes large.

"Yes," Liza quickly answered. "We grew up in the same area in Dakota." Her eyes were frosty even as her lips curled into a smile.

"That is very interesting," said Martina with an insincere smile toward Rebecca. She sat in the grandest, most comfortable chair in the room and motioned for the others to sit, as well. "You will have to fill us in on Rebecca's history. She seems determined to keep it a deep, dark secret from all of us."

Rebecca stiffened. "My history is very boring, I can assure you. I believe Liza's life would be more interesting to all of you."

Liza removed her gloves slowly, finger by finger.

"Rebel, I quite disagree with you. You have a very colorful past. So colorful, in fact, it might be hard to believe, but I promise all of you it is quite true." Liza arched a dainty eyebrow at Rebecca as if willing her to refute what she had to say.

"Tell me, Liza," Rebecca asked in an attempt to change the subject, "how is it that you come to be here?"

"I was invited to stay with Uncle Calvin and his

wife in Gaspar. There I met Jezreel and her husband, David. After I mentioned to them my old association with Cooper, they very kindly introduced me to Martina. Imagine my surprise when I heard about *you.* Little did I know, back then, you planned to worm your way into my beau's life. How a *creature* like you ever accomplished such a thing I will never understand. You must have used some type of sorcery."

Rebecca gasped at the vindictiveness Liza had unleashed. She'd spoken in a creamy, conversational tone, but her words were harsh. She'd become a pretty package of spite. Rebecca threw a glance at Jezreel's scornful face and knew she'd enlisted Liza in a campaign against her. Martina's countenance, smug and disdainful, seemed to prove it.

Liza gave a sly smile, turned to Chalina and continued. "Back home our little Rebel here was rather, um, *antisocial.* Quite the loner and very unwomanly. Her father was a half-breed, you know. She was snubbed by decent women."

Chalina had been struck speechless. She frowned with distaste at Liza as Jezreel smirked.

"Why would you say such hurtful things?" Her bow-shaped mouth hung open.

With narrowed eyes, Jezreel studied the portrait of Luke over the fireplace. Daisy entered, placidly unaware, balancing a tea tray on chubby arms.

"Daisy, we will have two supper guests this evening—you'll stay the night, will you not, ladies?" Martina looked quite pleased with herself.

"Thank you very much indeed, Mrs. Conrad," purred Liza. "You don't know how much I've looked forward to seeing my darling Cooper again."

Rebecca's face felt feverish; her temper flared. She was about to vent her blistering anger when she heard boots in the hall.

"It will be our pleasure to have you here." Martina said. "Speaking of my sons, I hear one of the boys coming in."

Cooper entered the room and stopped mid-stride, gaping at Liza as if she were an apparition. Rebecca could have toppled him with the wispiest touch of a feather duster. Her heart sank.

"Liza!" All Cooper's attention was for her.

Rebecca watched the scene unfolding before her, and she felt indignant, incensed, and most of all jealous.

Those women want a war.

Chapter Twenty

"Cooper, I'm sure you are surprised to see me," Liza cooed. "*Pleasantly* surprised, I hope." She stroked his muscular arm.

"I shouldn't be too astounded," he replied mildly. "Calvin told me he's your mother's brother. I never figured you'd come for a visit. Calvin and his wife aren't your cup of tea."

"Darling, when dear Uncle mentioned you in his letter of invitation, I just couldn't stay away." Liza opened her eyes wide in a transparent attempt to appear innocent, virtuous. "Your mother has kindly invited us to stay the night," she said silkily.

Across the room, Jezreel snickered. Chalina seemed unsure of what to say; she looked on diffidently.

Rebecca had been taken aback at Liza's acrimonious attitude toward her. Of the girls back home, Liza in all her glory had seemed one the nicest to her. It had to be jealousy making her act like this, going along with Jezreel, Rebecca thought. She really couldn't blame her, because, when it came to Cooper, she'd felt that same stab of rivalry herself. She felt it now, as she sat and silently watched them.

As Rebecca witnessed the reunion of Liza and

Cooper, everyone else in the room seemed to disappear. The two of them sat close together and reminisced cozily about the past in Yankton, the people they'd known there, and the gatherings they'd attended.

"Wasn't Rebecca attending these same functions?" Martina asked.

Cooper looked quickly at his wife then, as if he'd just remembered her existence.

"Rebel was far too busy to attend much of the merry-making in Yankton," he said in her defense.

"You don't need to make excuses for me," Rebecca said lightly, although her mood was far from light.

"I notice that both of you call her Rebel—that reminds me of 'Johnny Reb.' Were you anti-Union, Rebecca? A sympathizer for the Confederates?" Martina asked.

"My oldest brother was a Billy Yank," Jezreel broke in, her eyes narrowed and hostile. "He died under the command of George McClellan."

"The whole town called her Rebel," Liza said blithely. "She was a plow-chaser, you know, and such an unusual, rebellious girl. How my dear Cooper ever got mixed up with her, I have no idea." She began to stroke his arm again and she tweaked his ear.

Consternation shadowed Cooper's face.

"Now, look here—" he began.

"I'm sitting right here, Liza," Rebecca said tartly. "You're talking as if I weren't in the room."

"'Reb' is just a pet name that Cooper uses." Chalina's pretty face was clouded with concern and anxiety.

Cooper moved away from Liza's touch.

"I do use the name 'Rebel' as a pet name for Rebecca. 'Rebecca Marie LaRoche Conrad' is quite a mouthful to say."

"Your son, Mrs. Conrad, is such a gentle darling of

a man," Liza crooned. "He simply breaks all the girls' hearts. Especially mine."

She reached for Cooper's hand and captured it in both of hers.

Cooper reddened and scowled but left his hand lying limply in her grasp.

"I came in to tell you a small band of renegades has been sighted in the area," he said, perhaps to distract everyone from Liza's teasing. "They must be hungry. Some of the ranchers are missing beef. Make sure you travel with a guard, ladies. It could be dangerous for you out there on your journey home tomorrow. I've heard the natives are particularly fond of blondes. And look at what they did to Custer, Yellow Hair himself!"

"Cooper, is it safe for you boys to be out checking the cattle?" Martina asked.

"Should be fine, Mother. I've made it a rule that we all go out two by two."

"Oh, Cooper, darling, I feel faint with fright!" Liza said with guile in her voice and in her eyes. She cuddled closer and tightened her grip on his hand, obviously feigning alarm. She grabbed his rounded bicep with her free hand and clung to him.

Cooper extricated himself from Liza's clutches, peeling her off as he would leeches. He stood, looking reserved, taciturn.

"I'll send a couple of the boys into town to inform David and Calvin that the ladies are staying here tonight." He walked out of the room and out of the house.

Rebecca gave everyone a self-possessed glance as she rose to her feet.

"I believe Daisy could use some help preparing for this evening." She sedately sauntered from the room without a backward glance.

* * *

A shaft of rose-gold sunlight fell on the bed, warming Rebecca's bare legs. She had no wish or will to emerge from the cocoon of the bedroom and join the women below. Cooper had risen long before her, kissed her tenderly, and told her he had business to see to.

Now she heard voices below and caught fragments of the exchange: A man, perhaps Yago, gruffly announced that two bodyguards awaited, that the ladies' carriage was ready and they should be on their way.

At the top of the stairs now, tying her wrapper at the waist, Rebecca heard Martina below, objecting vociferously to the speed at which her company had been bustled out of the house.

"How rude of you," Martina scolded. "I did not raise my children to behave with such impudence as to hurry my company out like that! It was so obvious! It was Rebecca, wasn't it? She put you up to it, to get rid of them so quickly."

Yago must have had enough of his mother's carrying on. "Watch it, Mother. Reb is Coop's wife."

"What power has Rebecca got that everyone in this family wears blinders to who she really is?"

"And who is she, Mother?" It was Cooper, shouting angrily. Silence reigned for a few seconds.

Martina found her voice. "You heard what Liza said about her past. She's a half-breed! She's not our kind, she has no status." She sounded rattled, flustered.

"My wife may be the most honorable person in this house. Her father was a fine, noble person, and her mother, too. You want to know about Rebecca's past, just ask me and I'll tell you. You don't have to hear distorted versions from jealous women who aren't half what my wife is."

"Perhaps you are the one with the distorted view, my son." Martina countered. "I think Liza and Jezreel are right. She is holding something over you."

"You're right, she does have a hold on me. She was always an enigma to me, a sweet mystery. When I moved to Yankton and first met her father, I thought he was one of the wisest, most fascinating men I'd ever known.

"Then I met his daughter, someone like him, who studied under him, someone with true American blood running through her veins. So small, so petite, yet so perfectly capable in her own way that she scared the hell out of me. I tried to deny my feelings for her, but I began loving her even then."

Rebecca's hand came to her throat. *He loved me way back then?* Her heart swelled. She wanted to race down into Cooper's arms. She could face anything now, even her mean-spirited mother-in-law. She'd just begun to descend the stairs when his next words stopped her.

"You think Liza comes from noble stock, but her father was no good. He lost all his money to drink and gambling. Liza's looking for a rich husband. She's a prowling feline, fool's gold, hard and brittle and false. She's not the real thing."

"She sure is prejudiced against Reb," Yago said with a snort of agreement. "I never heard anyone carry on so."

Rebecca stood paralyzed at the top of the stairs, still eavesdropping in spite of herself.

"Mother, you should never have encouraged those two hellcats," Cooper said. "I thought you were better than that."

"You're right, my son." Martina's voice quavered. "I was raised to be gracious and mannerly. It seems ever since Luke died, I've forgotten how to be civilized." She sighed heavily.

"You *haven't* changed, that's just it," Cooper said. "You held sway over my father, and now you want to control my life, too. You should trust my judgment."

"*Lo siento*, my son. I'm so sorry I hurt you."

"You'll have to apologize to Rebel personally. It must come directly from you." Cooper spoke resolutely.

* * *

Days later Rebecca still hadn't received an apology from Martina, but the stubborn woman's reluctance didn't surprise her. At least, Rebecca thought, the older woman seemed more subdued and civil. Perhaps she finally realized her son and his new bride were radiantly happy together and would remain so despite any efforts of hers to the contrary.

Rebecca was up early one cold morning, helping Daisy in the kitchen just as she'd done as a maid. She laughed inwardly when she found a sweet apple dumpling concealed in one of Daisy's hiding places. The old dear was still stashing delicacies, she thought fondly.

After breakfast, Cooper and his brothers went out with small groups of ranch hands to round up cows and calves. They wanted them bunched and brought in closer to the ranch headquarters until the renegades left the area.

Hours later, Chester burst through the front door of the ranch house in an eruption of cold air and labored breathing, shattering the silence. He hadn't bothered to knock.

Rebecca ran to the entrance, her skirts tangling about her legs. The moment she saw him bent over, winded, hands on trembling knees, she knew he brought bad news. Cold fear seeped into her bones. "What is it, Chester?"

Martina appeared, pale and anxious. "What's happened?"

Alarm filled the old cowhand's wizened face.

"Indians have Micah."

"Micah. *Madre de Dios*!" Martina sank to the floor, eyes rolling back in her head.

"Mama!" Chalina kneeled at her mother's side and held her.

Chester grabbed Rebecca's arm. "The new boy, Moody, came for help. Says the natives have Micah. Two of the other hands went down defending him. Moody weren't close enough to see if they were dead or alive." He gulped air.

"Where?"

"Up on the north ridge, Miz Rebecca. I sent two hands to find Coop, but he's way out in the west section—"

"Get me Buster, unsaddled. Now!"

Chester nodded and hurried to do as he'd been told.

"Chalina, I need your help." She darted upstairs with Chalina on her heels, leaving Martina dazedly sitting there. "I need to change. Help me get out of these clothes, quickly!" The women worked together frantically, their fingers flying at the tiny buttons.

Dressed in her father's clothes—they fit her more snugly now, but it hardly registered—Rebecca took a few precious minutes to paint designs on her face the way her father had showed her so long ago. With rouge and kohl she transformed herself into an untamed primitive.

She wrapped her whip around her waist and sprinted to the front porch. Chester awaited, holding Buster's reins in his callused hands. In one smooth motion she threw herself onto the sorrel's bare back. She urged him into a gallop and they were off, her loose brown hair flowing in the wind stream.

* * *

Rebecca brought the horse to a sliding halt near the

top of the ridge, dismounted and crept to the edge. She hunkered down, all her senses focused on the scene below. Near a grove of trees, jubilant braves whooped and danced with abandon. A string of mangy ponies grazed nearby. In the center of the clearing, a bonfire roared and crackled and popped.

Rebecca squinted and, through the fiery heat-shimmer, saw Micah sagging between two posts, tied by his hands to a cross pole. An icy shiver of fright gripped her. The boy's face seemed bloodless, as white as paper. Was he still alive?

Some of the warriors brandished shields and seemed to be boasting to one another. Rebecca realized with a jolt that several figures were women in deerskin dresses and leggings. Each one carried a lance.

She stifled a scream when one of them strode to Micah and poked at him with her weapon. His body jerked and he cried out.

Rebecca winced. At least he wasn't dead.

Behind her, Yago arrived with several men. They crept up stealthily.

"Rebel," he said quietly.

She didn't look up, but ordered in an undertone, "You stay here, Yago. No matter what happens, *you stay here.* Is that clear?" She threw him a sharp glance before she fluidly mounted Buster and walked the horse over the crest and down the incline.

A shrill cry pierced the air when she drew closer to the temporary encampment. "*Wan la wa!* Look!" The woman who'd raised the alarm was pointing at her. Angry-looking men froze in place when they saw her coming toward them. She had their full attention now.

The smell of wood-smoke filled her nostrils, stung her eyes. Several of the hostiles closed in and menaced her with their clubs. Heart-poundingly afraid, Rebecca held up her hand in greeting. Panic welled in her throat, threatening to choke her.

She slid from the horse's back and walked on, fighting to keep steady.

A knot of men parted before her and she saw her old friend, Little Bull, approach. Relief flooded into her at the sight of him, but she did nothing to acknowledge their former rapport.

From the other side of the fire, Micah turned his head stiffly and gasped when he recognized Rebecca. His bloodied, battered mouth opened and closed soundlessly. His eyes rolled in the grip of terror.

"What do you want of my family?" Rebecca said.

Little Bull stood straight and tall, imposing in tight buckskin leggings and a buckskin shirt decorated with paint, beads and quills. He wore a knife under his belt and a quiver of arrows on his back. His handsome, burnished face—prominent cheekbones, chiseled mouth, strong nose—had been spotted with red paint. His ink-black hair swung past his shoulders, long and straight.

"We are hungry and angry," he said, shaking a fist. "Your government, your Great Father, promised us food and blankets, but the red children have no blankets. The meat is rotten, filled with maggots. The flour is moldy."

Rebecca heard despair, saw it in his face.

"We are—" he paused and began again. "We were a people of peace. But white-eyes invaded our sacred *Paha Sapa*, the Black Hills, the center of everything that is. A place of prayer that holds the dust of our ancestors.

"The intruders took *Tatanka*, sometimes only for the tongue. The buffalo gave us food, clothing, moccasins. They provided fuel for our campfires, hides for our shelters, strings for our bows. Their bones became our tools. "

The grief in his black eyes pained Rebecca to her very soul.

Little Bull spoke again. "Trespassers have taken our lands and destroyed our families. We destroy their families now."

Alarm knifed into her—she felt her eyes go wide with it. Thoughts tumbled through her brain.

"Take five spotted buffalo as ransom for the boy," she said.

"No, that will not do."

"Five spotted buffalo and me in place of the boy."

She stole a quick glance at Micah. His eyes were glazed, unfocused. Bright crimson gashes flowed freely from several wounds on his arms and legs.

"This we will do," Little Bull said, nodding. He spoke briefly to his men and gestured toward Micah.

Two braves untied the boy, slung his arms over their shoulders and dragged him before her. He sagged between them, ashen-faced. A moan escaped his swollen lips and a sheen of sweat coated his pale skin. Rebecca smelled coppery blood and acrid fear.

"Go," she told Micah. "Take Buster and go."

"Aren't you c-coming?" he asked.

"You go to your brother and tell him you need five fat steers. Have him bring them here, and then the men must leave. No matter what happens, they leave."

She motioned to the two warriors, nodding toward the sorrel's back, and they boosted the boy up. Buster snorted and shifted nervously under him.

"Reb? What you gonna do, Reb?" Micah's words were slurred with pain.

Rebecca drew a quavering breath and hollered at him. "Leave, now!" She slapped the horse on the rump.

Micah leaned forward, gripped Buster's mane, and galloped toward the top of the ridge.

Rebecca breathed a sigh of relief to see him reach the crest. Several cowhands surrounded him there and helped him off the horse.

* * *

Cooper and a hired hand had been searching for cows through heavy brush when they'd heard two riders coming at a fast clip. The cowboys drew rein when they reached him, their horses lathered and breathing hard.

"A band of Sioux raiders took Micah!" shouted the young ranch hand. "Two men who were with him are hurt, maybe dead."

Cooper's heart lurched, plummeted. "Where?"

"By the ridge, north, not too far from the ranch."

Fear for his loved ones surged through him. He raced off, trailed by the other men. He felt as if his insides were clumped into a monstrous knot. His heart knocked in his chest faster than the tempo of the horses' hooves.

* * *

The minutes crept by and Little Bull began stalking about, eyes roving restlessly. He noticed the whip around Rebecca's waist and called for his own to be brought to him.

Rebecca kept herself still and watchful. Little Bull flipped his wrist, lashing his rawhide whip toward her face. It snapped within inches of her cheek. She didn't flinch. His dark eyes flickered in recognition of her bravery.

Just then several cowhands on horseback came thundering over the ridge driving five steers ahead of them. Natives gathered the cattle into a makeshift corral while the cowboys rode to safety.

Little Bull strode away, leaving Rebecca alone, unguarded, but she understood she remained a prisoner. He quietly conversed with several of his men, then approached her again, his intense eyes glinting.

"We will have a contest of the long arm that bites," he said. "If you win, you will be set free, but if you lose," he smiled, "you will become my woman."

"*Han.* Yes," Rebecca said. But she had no intention of losing.

They separated themselves from the others and began. The spectators formed a large circle around them, vocalizing freely. Arms flashed and the snap of both whips rang out. Little Bull's first strikes were tentative, but they connected, biting, stinging her flesh. Rebecca felt small welts rising on her skin.

Some of the braves began taunting Little Bull and he grew more aggressive, pushing forward, compelling her to step back. Pain sliced into her, on her thighs, then her arms. Rebecca began fighting for her freedom.

Little Bull had learned much on his own, she thought, but her father had taught her many tricks. She began to bombard her powerful opponent with an onslaught of controlled strikes. The cracker of her bullwhip licked at his face and arms repeatedly. At the same time, Rebecca dodged his attacks. The sounds of their skirmish sliced through the air, cracks resounding like gunshots.

Winded, both of them panted now, circling each other.

Rebecca's nerve endings throbbed, her muscles strained. She flicked her wrist to wrap the whip tightly around Little Bull's neck, cutting off his air. When he sank to his knees and began to lose consciousness, she released him.

She'd ended it.

Now that it was over, her legs turned to jelly. She took a deep draught of the cool air and asked, "What will you and your people do now?"

Little Bull had regained his feet. He spoke in a low, sad tone. "We are going to the land far north, where we will be free. Goodbye, my friend. For the sake of others, you have faced danger courageously. We will speak of your *woohitika*, your courage, around our campfires."

Rebecca walked away carefully, feeling the sting of her wounds. When she crested the rise she stopped and turned to see that the Indians were already preparing to leave the area.

* * *

"Rebel!" Cooper raced to her side, took her into his arms, and held her tightly. She clung to him, sobbing, burying her face in his chest.

He'd arrived only minutes before to learn that it was his wife, not Micah, who was trapped in the midst of the savages below. Several of the hands had to hold him back to keep him from charging down there. Yago apprised him tersely of the developments. The hired hands released Cooper. By then, Rebecca was already making her way slowly up the hill.

"Micah's going to make it," Yago told him. "The other two will be all right, too."

When Cooper freed his wife from his trembling embrace, he saw with dismay that his hands were bloody. Her shirt was torn and wet with blood.

"My God, darling, what did they do to you?"

"It was a competition with the whip," Rebecca said.

"A contest?"

"I won freedom."

"What if the Indian had won?"

"I would have become Little Bull's woman."

Cooper went rigid.

"You went into that contest knowing this?" He stared at her in disbelief.

"Yes."

"If he had won . . . would you have signaled us for help?"

"I'd have had to honor my word and go with him."

His men were listening, silently gaping, watching to judge his reaction. Cooper felt his heart hammering, his face burning.

"Just like that?" He snapped his fingers in front of her face. "You would have gone just like that? Not even a struggle?"

"Yes. It was the only way to guarantee everyone's safety. I thank God that Little Bull was their leader."

"Little Bull wouldn't happen to be that heathen I saw you with once, would he?" Jealousy flared within Cooper.

"It was. I knew he couldn't bring it upon himself to really hurt me."

"Couldn't hurt you? What about this?" Cooper held up his bloodied palm. Anger and apprehension fought within him.

"He had to show the other warriors the contest was real."

Cooper had heard enough. He gave Rebecca a leg up on his horse, and she settled stiffly into the saddle. Cooper mounted behind her, holding her gingerly. "Let's get her home," he said to the others.

Chapter Twenty-One

"Dear Jesus!" Martina rushed from the veranda, her arms outstretched toward Cooper and Rebecca. "Is she hurt?"

Rebecca faltered, her legs rubbery, but she regained her footing. "N-not badly. How's Micah?"

The older woman's dark eyes were tearful and afraid, but her timid smile told Rebecca that Micah would be all right.

"He will recover," Martina said. "We sent for the doctor." She cocked her head at Rebecca, staring into her face.

"You risked yourself to save my son, after the shabby way I have treated you. I am *lo siento,* I very much regret the way I have been to you." She wiped away the wetness on her cheek.

"Forgive me, *por favor,* please," she said. Her sable eyes brimmed with sincerity.

"You're forgiven." Rebecca opened her arms and Martina hastened into them. "It's a wise woman who changes her mind," Rebecca said, smiling. "For a fool never will." She grinned and chuckled, and Martina laughed too.

"*Gracias, querida,*" Martina said.

Rebecca's heart lightened, as if someone had opened all the windows of a stuffy room to let in fresh air and sunlight. A warm glow suffused her.

Cooper had been watching the two of them with concern on his handsome face, but now his eyes danced with good humor. He took his wife from his mother's embrace into his own.

"You will hear nothing but praise from me from now on. I promise," Martina said. She looked deeply into Rebecca's eyes and Rebecca knew she meant every word.

Chester made his way toward them, his limping gait slowing him down. Cooper lifted his wife into his arms and called out to the old man.

"Get Blackie's special salve." He carried Rebecca into the house and up the stairs.

In their room, Cooper gingerly removed Rebecca's clothing and looked her over. He blanched at the sight of angry red welts and open cuts on her skin.

"Oh, my poor baby," he murmured.

There came a soft knock at the door, and Daisy entered with the salve, warm water and bandages. She hovered nearby, watching Cooper gently wash Rebecca's wounds and rub salve into them.

"We'll take our meals here for a day or two," he told Daisy. He turned back to Rebecca and brushed the fine strands of hair away from her face. He leaned in and tenderly kissed Rebecca's closed eyelids.

"Sleep, my Rebel wife," he whispered.

* * *

Cooper helped Rebecca down from the wagon, admiring her trim figure and polished charms. She'd tucked her gleaming brown locks under a bronze-colored bonnet for their jaunt into Gaspar. Cooper watched her reticule sway provocatively at her hip as she walked away. She amazed him. He would never tire of the many facets of her personality.

This woman will continue to surprise and delight me for the rest of my life.

When she reached the door of the general store, he called out, "I'll be down at the saddlery, need a new sole on my boot."

In the leather shop, Cooper waited patiently for his repair to be done. He breathed deeply of the pleasant smells of saddle soap and new boots. Finally he exited the building, just in time to bump into Jezreel.

She grabbed his arm and said, "I suggest, Cooper, darling, you keep that busy little wife of yours on a tighter leash." Her voice sounded razor sharp.

Cooper frowned and elevated one eyebrow. "What's that supposed to mean?"

"It means your goody-goody wife is at this moment entertaining my husband. I saw her go into his office arm-in-arm with him, and I don't like it."

"If you would give your husband a little more loving maybe he wouldn't go looking for it elsewhere."

"I should slap you for that."

"Everyone knows the two of you don't get on, Jezreel."

"You know nothing of my husband or my marriage." Her lips thinned with indignation.

Cooper spun on his heel and left the angry woman behind him. He felt thunderous inside, and perhaps jealous, too. Then it occurred to him that maybe Rebecca was speaking with David about his birth mother, Tillie. Rebecca had shared the secret that the owner of the Inn was David's true parent. She hadn't answered when Cooper had inquired about the father. Cooper's sense of rivalry cooled as he strolled to David's office certain that was what they were discussing.

"—and I plan to spend a week in Promise, getting

to know her better," David was saying.

Cooper approached the desk and took a seat beside his wife.

"She'll like that, David," Rebecca said, beaming at both men in turn. "And so will you, I assure you."

David leaned over, took Rebecca's hand into his and squeezed.

"So! This is cozy." Jezreel stamped into the room with a sneer on her lips and an accusing glare. She turned her outrage toward Rebecca. "You keep your grasping hands off my David!"

"Jezreel!" David stared at her with wide eyes, stunned by his wife's streak of possessiveness.

"There is nothing going on between us except friendship," Rebecca said.

"Don't you dare try to send him secret messages with your wicked green eyes." Jezreel's voice dripped with acid. "You may be able to pull such pranks with Cooper, but you won't get by with it around me!"

David's stoicism dissolved in a burst of amusement. Jezreel's face was dark with shock.

Rebecca looked at him and she began to smile. Cooper, too, caught the contagion.

Jezreel grimaced at Cooper and slapped at his arm.

"You stupid fool, there is no joke!" She faced her husband. "What's so funny?"

"Rebecca and I are not having an affair," David said. "Get that notion out of your head right now."

Jezreel's gaze veered between the three of them. "If you aren't lovers, then there's something else going on and I want to know what it is."

"Yes, there is something," Cooper said. He looked from David to Rebecca and saw his wife squirm in her seat.

"It's nothing to do with Rebecca and me," David said, loosening his collar. "Don't badger your wife, Cooper. It's not her place to say."

Jezreel said nothing, but watched her husband intently.

"There's a woman in Promise, Rebecca's good friend Tillie who's my real mother." He paused while Jezreel absorbed the information. Then his eyes met Cooper's and held, and he pressed on, "Tillie and your father were, at one time . . . lovers."

"And you are their son." Cooper said, finally understanding.

David nodded. Everyone in the room waited soundlessly.

"Well, that explains a lot. Brother."

"Rebecca helped me understand I was taking it out on you for the wrong reasons.You were just as innocent as I was," David said. "She wanted to tell you sooner, Cooper, " he pushed his thick fair hair off his forehead, "but I wasn't ready."

Cooper studied David's athletic figure and pleasantly rugged face. "I can't believe no one realized it sooner. You and Micah look so much alike. Did Father know?"

"No. Maybe. I'm not sure."

"What about Martina?" Jezreel broke in, sounding anxious. "Does she know?"

"She doesn't have to know," David said. "It's ancient history."

"Well, not for me," Jezreel said. "What about our share of the inheritance?"

"Leave it to you to bring up money," David said, shaking his head. "The money was Martina's to begin with. It remains with her children."

Jezreel opened her mouth to argue with him, but David was ready for it.

"If you say one word about this, so help me, Jezreel, I will divorce you," he said solidly.

"David, you wouldn't." Tears began to well in her eyes, but they seemed to have no effect on her usually-pliant husband.

"I've had enough of your scheming. Everyone has had enough of your scheming. From now on you *will* behave yourself, and you will treat me, your loving husband, with the respect I deserve."

Jezreel stood stock still, her mouth open, her eyes blinking rapidly. Cooper thought he detected a freshly-minted regard, a new admiration for her husband, coming over her.

"Now," David said, and he drew a great breath. "Let's go home where you can act out in privacy."

Rebecca, smiling, turned toward Cooper, grabbed his arm and gave him a hug.

"I love you, Cooper Conrad."

He looked into her eyes of melted jade.

"Shall we head home, too, where we can act out in private?"

* * *

They drove in silence for awhile, with only the creaking of the wagon to accompany their thoughts. Rebecca assumed that Cooper was mulling over the news about David's true parentage. She didn't want to disturb him with idle chatter. It took her by surprise when he introduced a new subject.

"I heard about a new breed of cattle that's been brought over from Scotland. I'd like to add some to our breeding stock. Virgil has imported them."

"Virgil. He's—"

"Let me guess. 'He's a good friend of mine.' Is that what you were going to say?" Cooper stopped the wagon and turned to look Rebecca squarely in the eyes.

"I suppose he would qualify as an old suitor."

"Ah yes. The Virgil of the letter. Let me think, how did that go? 'You will always have a large part of my heart.' You know, until I read that, I thought the only competition I had was that Indian and the bird-legged cowhand at Tillie's."

Rebecca giggled at Cooper's absurd description of Patrick. "Oh, that reminds me." she said, "In the general store today, Calvin told me Liza has gone to stay in Promise for a spell." She suppressed another titter. "It seems she'd heard there were some prosperous young bachelors there."

Cooper's eyes gleamed with merriment. "You laugh now. You didn't think it so funny when she had her mitts on me, did you?"

Rebecca gave his arm a squeeze

"How would you feel about a house of our own, down in the hollow by the creek?" She studied his strong, handsome profile, gauging his reaction. "Martina has been more than pleasant. It's not about that."

Cooper, eyes closed, held his face toward the warmth of the sun.

"She's been downright sweet, hasn't she?" He sounded amazed.

"Building a new home would complete the circle, do you see, my love?" It all came back to her then, dreadful memories of ruin and death. "It's how we came together, the loss of my home." She yanked her hat off and allowed her hair to tumble free. "We can afford it, too. I'm a rich woman, remember?"

He turned to her with that familiar intensity on his features, the hypnotizing eyes that made her feel quivery inside.

"I want a place of our own, too. Just the two of us, at first, anyway." His quick smile told her what he was thinking, and her heart thrilled. He wrapped his arm around her, pulling her to his powerful chest, kissing the top of her head. "My brown-haired beauty," he said.

"Mmm. To grow things with my own two hands

again, to feed our children with the harvest—I can't wait!"

Cooper flicked the reins and they started toward home again, at a faster clip than before.

Rebecca gazed at her husband, smiling with contentment as her heart swelled, filled to overflowing.

He looked back at her with simmering passion. "If you ever glanced at another man with that love in your eyes, it would kill me."

"I could say the same about you looking at another woman."

"Life is meaningless without the right person," he said, taking her hand. "You're my affinity, my soul, my center."

She searched his face and knew this man would always be her blessing, her life's partner. Her heartland.

She remembered their journey from Dakota Territory nearly three years before. *Together we've embarked on another odyssey, making our own family.* Suddenly, though she sat close to Cooper on the wagon, it wasn't enough. Rebecca felt the pressing need to be even closer to him. The ranch was far away. A grove of pines near the road beckoned to them, with its grass carpet and thick shrubbery. The day was splendid; there was no one around for miles.

The vegetation cradled them where they lay, patches of golden light filtering down upon them. Their hearts beat with the same cadence, bodies pulsed to the same rhythm.

Long moments later they lay naked and sated in each other's arms. They inhaled the resinous scent of the pines and listened to the birds calling. A warm, fresh breeze ruffled the grasses; bees hovered around roadside flowers. The cycle of seasons, the phases of the moon, the recurring sequences of nature. They were all part of a great pattern. Sweet peace filled her.

"'Love burns like a blazing fire . . . many waters cannot quench it.' It's from the Song of Songs," she said.

Cooper leaned over and kissed her fervently. "That's right, my Rebel, my love. It does burn. Hot, strong, and forever."

LYNN DELL
BIO

Paula Guhin (blonde) is half of Lynn Dell, pen name for the two authors of *Dakota Rebel.* She writes happily from her home in Aberdeen, South Dakota, where she is the mother of seven Arabian horses and an assortment of dogs and cats. She is the author of *Glorious Glue, Art with Adhesives* (J. Weston Walch), *Can We Eat the Art?* (Incentive Publications), and *The King of Corn* (Prairie Home Press).

Dell Kleinsasser (brunette), also half of Lynn Dell, lives in Freeman, South Dakota with her husband. She is an accomplished artist and writer who has two grown daughters.

CALLING ALL READERS!

VISIT NEW AGE DIMENSIONS ONLINE

Our readers are special to us so we've made our website very reader friendly. You can get the scoop on your favorite New Age Dimensions authors while keeping up to date with our imprints and lines. While you're on the web you can:

Read excerpts.

View covers of scheduled releases.

Read about our authors and staff.

Enter contests as we run them.

Purchase our releases as an eBook or Trade Paperback directly from our site on secure servers.

View our online catalog.

Join our groups where you can message or chat with us.

Visit our forum.

Check out our calendar.

Get the latest news.

Email us!

Visit us online today at:

http://www.NewAgeDimensionsPublishing.com